JETT'S GUARD

A BASTARDS AND BADGES NOVEL

ANDI RHODES

Copyright © 2020 by Andi Rhodes

All rights reserved.

No part of this book may be reproduced in any form or by any electronic or mechanical means, including information storage and retrieval systems, without written permission from the author, except for the use of brief quotations in a book review.

Cover Artwork – © 2020 L.J. Anderson of Mayhem Cover Creations

For Diana - I appreciate your support and love more than I can say. Not only are you my step-mom, you're my friend. Thank you for always being willing to lend an ear or a shoulder but more than that, thank you for loving my dad.

ALSO BY ANDI RHODES

Broken Rebel Brotherhood

Broken Souls

Broken Innocence

Broken Boundaries

Broken Rebel Brotherhood: Complete Series Box set

Broken Rebel Brotherhood: Next Generation

Broken Hearts

Broken Wings

Broken Mind

Bastards and Badges

Stark Revenge

Slade's Fall

Jett's Guard

Soulless Kings MC

Fender

Joker

Piston

Greaser

Riker

Trainwreck

Squirrel

Gibson

Satan's Legacy MC

Snow's Angel

Toga's Demons

Magic's Torment

He walked into my heart like he always belonged there, took down my walls and lit my soul on fire.
- T. M.

PROLOGUE

JETT

"Are you sure about this?"

I study Jackson and Slade for a moment before returning my attention to Special Agent in Charge, Timothy Bing. Based on the scowls on their faces, they aren't happy about needing help, but it would be impossible for them to do the job without being recognized.

"I'm sure." I flip through the pages of the file in front of me. "This guy was a cop?"

"A detective," Slade sneers.

"Damn," I mutter.

According to the file, Jeffrey Lee is currently serving a life sentence in a federal prison for human trafficking, kidnapping, attempted murder and fraud, among other things. He's also the biological son of Saul Luciano, a man that I, along with Jackson and Slade, put away last year. None of us knew about Jeffrey at the time, which makes sense considering he was given up for adoption at birth.

"How long will I be undercover?"

"As long as it takes," SAC Bing reports. "Obviously, this isn't the type of thing we'd normally get involved in as Lee's crimes aren't drug related, but, other than these two," he nods to indicate Jackson and Slade. "You have the most knowledge about the family and their operations. And Lee has never seen you, so it'll be easier for you to get what we need."

"And what exactly is it that we need?"

"We now know that Lee, alongside Sapphire and her father, had started to expand their *enterprise* across the country. We need you to get close to Lee and get him to open up to you, tell you who else is involved and locations of where they're housing the women."

"This guy was a detective. What makes you think he won't smell an undercover agent from a mile away? Clearly he knows how to blend in. I assume that also means he's more astute than this operation gives him credit for."

"Six months ago, that may have been the case, but he suffered massive injuries during the explosion that killed Sapphire, his biological sister. During interrogations, his memories seem to remain intact, but he's not firing on all cylinders."

"That doesn't necessarily make me feel better. If anything, that may make him more dangerous."

"Listen, Jett, if we didn't think you could handle it, we wouldn't have requested you," Jackson says. "I worked alongside you for a year, and I never had a clue that you were DEA. And I'm a damn good agent. If you fooled me, you can fool Jeffrey Lee."

I lean back in my chair and interlock my fingers behind my head. Lee seems to be a chip off the old block despite being adopted and raised by two loving parents who had nothing to do with the criminal underworld of his biological family. While he personally isn't going to be hurting anyone from a jail cell, that doesn't mean there aren't others on the outside that will on his and the Luciano family's behalf.

Images of the concrete rooms that housed the victims of this particular family flash through my mind. Katelyn and Brandie, the fiancés of Jackson and Slade respectively, were among the women taken and tortured by the Luciano's. The conditions were beyond disgusting, and each was degraded and treated like lesser beings than cockroaches. My stomach rolls at the thought of what they went through.

"What's my backstory?" I ask, leaning forward and resting my forearms on my knees.

SAC Bing slide's another file across the table. "It's all in there. We kept as much of your actual personal history as we could the same, to make it easier on you. You're in prison following a drug raid."

I skim through the words on the pages, and blood whooshes through my ears. I get tunnel vision as the details of my life before the DEA haunt me. I've always known, on some level, that the specifics weren't a secret, but to have it confirmed and used as part of an operation is unsettling.

"Will I have a contact in the prison?" I ask SAC Bing after slamming the file closed. I make a point of not looking at Jackson and Slade, unable to handle whatever pity I know will be on their faces.

"No. With Lee being former law enforcement, we don't want to take the chance that he's already got someone on the inside. No one there will know your true identity. I'll be your only point of contact. I'll visit you once a week, as your attorney, and you can call me when you're permitted phone calls."

"Jett, listen," Slade straightens in his chair. "I'd give anything to go in your place. Lee is bad news, and this isn't going to be easy. I'm not saying you can't handle it. It's just…" He scrubs his hands over his face in frustration.

"I think what he's trying to say is that this is going to be a lot different from our time undercover at The White Lily," Jackson explains. "We still had our freedom then. In prison, not only are you completely stuck, but you're also going to be in close proximity to some of the worst criminals there are. Your safety will be at risk every single day, and nine times out of ten, the threats to you won't be because of this case."

I shove up from my chair and start to pace the office. "Got it. It's going to be dangerous. I'm not some newbie agent that isn't fully aware of the risks." I pick up my cover story file. "In case you missed it, nothing in my life has been easy. I don't do *easy*." I tuck the folder under my arm and stride to the door. With my fingers wrapped around the knob, I glance over my shoulder. "When do I leave?"

"You'll be traveling to Washington state with Slade when he returns home. He'll handle getting things set up so you're on the first available transport from the local jail to the federal prison."

"Brandie and I have a flight back tonight. I already have your ticket. We'll pick you up at four-thirty, on our way to the airport."

"Then if you'll excuse me, I've got some things to take care of."

I yank open the door and make my way out of the building. I don't grab anything from my office because I won't need any of that where I'm going.

I review the operation in my head, over and over, while I make the necessary phone calls to make sure my rental home is packed up and belongings put in storage while I'm gone. I know from my time undercover before that SAC Bing will make sure that everything is handled properly and there are no loose ends.

Over the next forty-eight hours, I debate on calling my parents, letting them know I'm going to be out of touch for a while. I don't make the call though. They haven't given a shit about me in a long time. Hell, they hadn't even noticed that I'd been out of touch the last time.

When I step onto the bus transport, my hands and legs shackled, I shift my thoughts from my past to the task at hand. I've spent a lot of time in prisons, but never as a criminal. I'm not worried about being able to handle myself or keep any actual threats to my safety at bay.

I take in the few other prisoners around me. One guy looks like he's jonesing for his next fix, and another looks like he could use a hug from his mommy. A third guy is staring straight ahead, giving no indication that he's even aware that there are people around him. And the fourth guy looks like he could be my grandfather. If this is a representation of what lies ahead for me, I'll be just fine.

The bus slows to a stop, and a look out the window tells me we've arrived. For as far as I can see, there's barbed wire fencing atop what appear to be roughly twenty-foot-tall concrete walls. When we pass through the gates, I get my first glimpse of my new home. It's a goddamn fortress.

"We're here," the guard at the front of the bus says as he stands up. "Get your asses up and moving. We don't got all day."

I slowly walk down the center aisle of the transport. I'm the last prisoner to exit, and when I do, I'm immediately struck with a sense of dread. There are inmates lined up against the fence, catcalling and shouting at us. Some are sticking their tongues through the chain link fence and wiggling them in a suggestive manner.

The four others from the bus are definitely *not* an accurate representation.

When it's my turn to walk through the metal detectors to enter the prison, I hesitate for a moment. I'm shoved forward with something hard against my back and stumble when the chain between my ankles reaches its limit.

When I gain my balance, I notice the guard behind me holding a nightstick. His name tag identifies him as Officer Cox and the shit-eating grin on his face tells me he's someone I need to watch my back with.

He leans toward me and is inches from my face when he says, "Welcome to hell, *inmate*."

1

EMMA

Two years later...

"What're ya gonna do without your bitches, Lee?"

Lee shoots Stu a glare that most men would cower under, but not Stu Cox. Stu is a fellow guard at the prison and uses his position to his advantage any chance he gets. He has zero respect for the inmates under his watch, and Lee is currently his target.

"With a name like *Cox*, maybe I'll make you my bitch."

Stu's elbow connects with Lee's face, and his head flies back, blood spurting from his nose. I've seen this happen more times than I can count, and I roll my eyes at Stu's display of machismo. There are just some inmates that you don't mess with, and Lee is one of them.

I pull a Kleenex out of my pocket and try to hand it to Lee to clean up his face. Rather than take it from me, he raises his brow and smirks.

"I can handle a little blood, Miss Jordan." His gaze drops to my chest, and he licks his lips, not caring about the crimson drops.

Lee may not take shit from the other guards, but he is always respectful to me. It's probably because he thinks if he butters me up, he may get something other than prison pussy, but that's never going to happen. I may be going through a dry spell, but I'm not desperate enough to let my inmates get a piece of me.

"Eyes forward, Lee," I demand, injecting as much authority into my voice as I can.

Like Lee, most prisoners don't give me too much of a hard time, but it hasn't always been like that. I became a guard at the age of twenty-five and being a female in a male-dominated field always comes with its challenges. Add in the fact that I'm pretty petite with a big rack and most don't take me too seriously. What respect I do get, I take and don't look too closely at the motives. If I did, I'd lose my mind.

"Aw, Miss Jordan, you're ruining my fun."

"Lee, shut it before I sh—"

Lee yanks out of my hold and faces Stu. "Before you what?"

"Lee!" I shout, my hand going to my taser in case things get out of control.

Lee looks over his shoulder at me and says, "Sorry Miss Jordan."

I have no time to figure out what he means because the next thing I know, he's drawing back his fist and his elbow connects with my eye socket. Pain radiates through my skull, but I ignore it and move in closer to try to stop him from beating Stu to a bloody pulp, even though he might deserve it. Lee isn't letting a little thing like shackles slow him down, and Stu's more bark than bite so things aren't going well for him.

That's my last thought before lights out.

The beeping noise has to stop. I try to open my eyes and figure out where it's coming from, but the light is blinding so I slam them shut. Thinking it's my cell phone's alarm and that I'm going to be late for work, I feel around for the device, intent on silencing it.

"Hey, Doc. I think she's waking up."

Who the fuck is that?

"Emma? Emma, are you awake?"

I know that voice.

Thankfully, the beeping stops but the light gets brighter, despite not opening my eyes.

"Quit shining that damn thing in her face and maybe she could answer you?"

"I'm a doctor, Storm. I think I know how to do my job." The light dims so I slowly lift my lid, resisting the urge to squeeze them shut. I need to figure out what's going on, and I can't do that if I can't see.

I glance around the room, take in the hospital style beds and cabinets full of medical supplies. I'm in the prison infirmary, and I have no idea why.

"Len?" I sit up, ignoring the throbbing in my head, and swing my legs over the edge of the bed I'm in. "What happened?"

"You don't remember?" he asks just as he shines that damn light in my eyes again.

"Would you stop that?" I swat at his hand. "It fucking hurts."

"Sorry, Emma. Just trying to make sure you don't have a concussion."

A flash of memory hits, but it's just a glimpse. Stu and I

walking Lee to solitary. Lee being a dick. Nothing too out of the ordinary.

"Why would I have a concussion?"

"You got cold-cocked by an inmate. You've been out for a while."

"Oh, well, I'm awake now."

I stand and the room spins. I reach behind me to steady myself, and when the dizziness eases, I take a step. I immediately collapse, barely missing getting up close and personal with the floor. Len catches me but seems to struggle under my weight. I'm a hundred and thirty pounds soaking wet, so clearly he doesn't work out.

"Back in bed, inmate," Len barks.

I look over my shoulder to see Storm straining against the cuffs that have him attached to the bed. He's in prison-issued blue scrub pants, but instead of the matching shirt required of all prisoners, he's sporting a white bandage with a growing red stain. His muscles are bunching, but his face is pale.

"What're you in for?" I ask as Len helps me back onto the bed.

"Read my file and you'd know." Storm sits back on his own bed, rubbing his bare chest and scowling at his covered wound.

"No, I don't mean the reason you're in prison." I close my eyes and breathe through my nose to counteract the nausea. "Why are you bleeding like a stuck pig?"

Storm snorts and a small smile plays on my lips. "Well, my cellie didn't take too kindly to me pointing out that he should brush his teeth more. Shivved me with a toothbrush."

"Damn." I roll my head to look at him. "Gotta appreciate the irony, though."

"I guess. Seriously, his teeth are already yellow. Now they're gonna rot."

"Didn't think that one through too much, did he?"

"Nope." I watch as he touches his bandage and winces.

"Hey, Len?" I lift my head and search for the doctor, but he's nowhere to be seen. "Len!" I shout.

It takes a moment, but he comes through the door and quickly makes his way to my bedside.

"Yeah, Emma?"

I tilt my head toward Storm. "Your patient's hurting. Can't you give him anything for the pain?"

Len's eyes narrow as he frowns.

"I'm fine." Storm's tone is gruff, and he sounds nothing like the guy that was just joking around with me.

Len completely ignores Storm and focuses his attention on me.

"So, Emma, I was wondering, would you like to grab a drink after work?"

His eyes light up, like they do every time he asks me out. He's forever bound to be disappointed. I don't date co-workers, and he's not my type so the answer is always the same.

"Thanks, Len, but I'm going to have to pass. Maybe some other time." I know that the answer is more encouraging than it should be, but I'm not a bitch. And I have to work with him so no need to make things uncomfortable.

"Oh, right. Yeah, maybe another time." Len takes a step back. "You should try to relax. I'll keep an eye on the inmate and make sure you aren't disturbed. A few hours of rest and you should be good to go."

"I'm not worried about Storm. Do what you need to do."

Storm lets out another snort, and Len's narrowed eyes are back. I close mine to block out the two of them, but they fly open when the prison alarms start blaring.

"What the hell is that?" Storm shouts to be heard over the siren.

"Riot alarm," I yell as I jump up and shove the dizziness away.

I know we don't have much time before a horde of pissed off prisoners reach the infirmary, and I need to secure the area. I glance at Storm and see him struggling against his restraints, but he's going to have to continue to struggle. No way am I letting him loose.

I've been trained on what to do during a riot and assumed that everything would be automatic if I ever needed it. I also assumed that there'd never be a reason to actually *need* the training. I was wrong on both counts.

Fuck!

Needing to do something, anything, I begin to bark out orders.

"Len, I need you to barricade the door. When you're done with that, I need you to gather anything and everything that could be used as a weapon and pile them here on the bed."

I run to the cabinets and start to grab syringes, vials of medicine, rubbing alcohol, basically I snatch it all. Len is rooted to the same spot he was when the alarm first sounded, and his eyes are comically round.

"Len! Snap out of it."

I go to him, shake him out of his stupor. His eyes are wide, but he seems to bolster himself and begins to help. He manages to get a few exam tables pushed in front of the door, and together we lift filing cabinets on top of them to block the window.

"Those aren't going to keep these guys out," Storm says from his perch on the bed. He's no longer straining to get free but rather is sitting there, calmly taking in our actions.

As if to punctuate his warning, our barricade rattles as the rioters pound on the door. I automatically reach for my taser and wince when it's not in its usual holster. It must have been taken after I was knocked out. I recognize Lee's face through the glass, and his sneer sends a shiver through me.

Glass breaks and our pitiful barrier crumbles, piece by piece. I turn around and reach for a syringe and vial, anything that could potentially slow these animals down. Just as I puncture the rubber cap with the needle, hands lock around my throat.

"I've been dying to get my hands on you," a threatening voice growls next to my ear. *Lee!*

The bottle falls to the ground and shatters as I reach up and scratch the hands that are choking the life out of me. My eyes lock with Storm's, and his seem cold, dead. There is nothing in him to indicate that there's a shred of decency within.

"Keep it up. I like my bitches with a little fight in them." Lee grinds his pelvis against me, and his erection only adds credence to his statement.

Black spots dance in my vision, and breathing becomes almost impossible. I don't think Lee will kill me, not if he likes the fight, but I have a feeling that I'll wish I was dead when he's done with me. He drags me toward the wall and turns me so I can watch the chaos and destruction.

I notice that Len is still in one piece, and before I can even wonder why, I see him handing over whatever drugs are demanded of him. He's not even resisting, and it dawns on me that he hasn't done a single thing to try to help me. He's only interested in helping himself. *Asshole.* Doesn't he get it? They'll kill him as soon as they're done with him.

Realizing that I have no chance in hell of making it out of here alive, I quit fighting. I'd rather Lee just kill me than play with me first. I force the tension to leave my body, and his grip loosens. I suck in giant gulps of air, my throat and lungs burning.

Lee steps around to face me, bending down to stare into

my eyes. I try to keep my fear hidden from him, school my expression as much as possible. His eyes narrow and then he backhands me, splitting my lip. I drop my chin and run my tongue over the cut, wincing at the sting.

When I don't react the way he wants, he backhands me again, this time catching the corner of my eye. I thrust out my chin and let a smile form, refusing to give him what he wants. He wraps his fist in my hair and slams my head against the wall. Once. Twice. If I didn't have a concussion before, I definitely have one now.

"Fight me, bitch!" Spit flies from his mouth.

"Jesus, do what he tells you." Storm's pleading command reaches my ears, and I roll my eyes to look at him. His jaw is set, his eyes are slits of anger, and his muscles are bunching from him straining to break free.

Now he wants to help?

Next thing I know, I'm on my back on the tiled floor, staring up at Lee as he straddles me. His hands are rough when he gropes me through my shirt. I let my head fall to the side, needing to distance myself from the situation. Fingers grip my chin as he forces me to look at him, and with his free hand, Lee undoes my belt buckle and rips my pants open. He lets go of my chin and yanks my shirt, the buttons flying off and clinging to the floor.

He bares my chest, and heat scorches my cheeks. Cold air hits my legs before Lee's weight settles on top of me. He frees his dick and fists himself, stroking a few times. I squeeze my eyes shut and conjure up images of my family. They all warned me of the dangers of this job, and I blew them off, didn't take them seriously. I wish I would have.

My eyes fly open as something clangs to the floor across the room. Lee raises his arm to backhand me, but another hand grips his wrist mid swing and stops his assault. A growl escapes Lee as he's hauled off of me and I'm free. I scramble into a sitting position, scooting toward the corner and wrapping my arms around my knees.

Storm somehow managed to break out of his cuffs, and he's wailing on Lee with controlled blows. At first, Lee fights back, but eventually, he seems to recognize that it's a fight he won't win and his window of opportunity for escape is closing, so he takes off out the door. Storm glances around the room before stalking toward me. I cower closer to the wall, whimpering. When he crouches next to me and reaches a hand out toward my face, I flinch.

"I'm not going to hurt you." His voice is deep, his face a mask of determination.

I don't say anything, just sit there, staring at him, trying to determine if he can be trusted. Out of the corner of my eye, I see Len, lying on the floor, bleeding from a head wound. He's likely dead, not that he was much help anyway. Then I notice that the other inmates are no longer in the room. Dozens of them are running down the hall, yelling as they go, trying to get to freedom. The sound of gunshots registers, and I don't know if it's the other guards or if the prisoners managed to gain control of all the weapons.

"C'mon. We need to get you outta here." Storm scoops me up, and before I can stop myself, I wrap my arms around his neck.

He carries me to the door, or rather to the hole in the wall where the door used to be. Rethinking his strategy, he whirls and goes to the bed to grab a blanket and, while holding me with one arm, covers my entire body.

"I know you're scared, but I need you to be as quiet as possible." Storm's hot breath penetrates the flimsy material when he whispers in my ear.

I nod, knowing I don't have any other choice. He's either going to kill me or save me. If he's going to save me, then it's in my best interest to listen. If he's going to kill me, then it doesn't matter what I do.

We're moving, quickly, and with each step Storm takes, a jolt of pain shoots through my body. I can see shadows moving behind the blanket and I can hear everything going on around me, but I have no idea what exactly that is.

"Damn, Storm, what'd you do?" I recognize the voice, but the name of its source isn't coming to me.

"Bagged me a guard," Storm replies and his tone is so matter of fact that I almost scream out. Remembering that he told me to be quiet, I bite my lip, holding my fear in.

"Well, shit. You might want to avoid this exit then. Cops are everywhere out there. You wanna get outta here, not get snagged for murder."

Don't avoid this exit! Take me to the cops! I'll tell them that you rescued me. That you had nothing to do with the riot.

Storm's fingers dig into my skin, silently begging me to relax, and that's when I realize my body stiffened. I force the tension away, hoping that his friend doesn't notice.

"Thanks, man, but I think I'll take my chances. Too many enemies the other direction."

"Good luck." The guy chuckles. "Look me up on the outside. Maybe we can make some coin together."

"I'll do that."

Storm's walking again, and he leans his head closer to me to whisper, "Sorry about that."

The more steps he takes, the brighter it gets beyond the blanket. Within minutes, a strong wind lifts the corner of the blanket, letting me know we're outside. There's shouting and footsteps all around me, along with the sound of guns being cocked. They're yelling at Storm to put me down and drop to his knees with his hands behind his head.

He lays me on the ground and removes the blanket. I watch as he does what he's told. With his fingers interlaced behind his head, he glances down at me and gives a small smile.

"Told you I'd get you outta there." His arms are yanked behind him as an officer slaps cuffs over his wrists. He's hauled to his feet, and as he's being led away, he glances at me over his shoulder. "Name's Jett."

2

JETT

"Good morning, rock heads. That was Def Leppard and I'm Jerri, here to bring you the best…"

The woman on the radio has a raspy voice and it sounds nothing like the one that I've dreamt about every night since the riot. As Jerri's voice fades into another song, I sit up and rub a fist into my chest and stare at the white sheets twisted around my legs.

My undercover operation ended a week ago. Jeffrey Lee managed to escape during the chaos of the riot, and I had to spend another two weeks in prison after that to ensure my cover wasn't blown in case he was caught. He wasn't, so I was 'released'. The FBI has taken over the case and will continue to search for him while I shift my focus back to my duties with the DEA.

I unwind my legs and swing them over the edge of the mattress, letting my feet hit the carpeted floor and my toes sink into the shaggy fibers. I'm staying in a cheap motel while I search for another apartment. I gave up mine before going undercover, and while I'm ready for a home, I want it to be exactly what I want and not something I settle for.

The noises from the other motel guests seep through the paper-thin walls, and I tune them out. My living arrangements are temporary, and after having spent so much time in a prison, I can handle pretty much anything.

As I stare at the motel wall, I review the phone call I received from my parents' attorney yesterday. Both of my parents died in a car accident while I was undercover, and the attorney had to wait to review their will with me. From what he said, they left me everything, but I have no idea what that even means. I grew up in a family that was loaded, but it's been so long since I even talked to the people who raised me that, for all I know, they could have died broke.

I make my way to the shitty bathroom, clean clothes and toiletries in hand, and lock the door behind me. The water takes too long to heat up, so I step under the spray and let the cold hit my skin. My eyes slide closed as memories assault me of other cold showers, ones I hadn't been alone to take. I turn around in the stall and tip my head back to rinse the soap off of my face. The water finally warms as I finish scrubbing the shampoo through my too-long hair.

Now that the water isn't frigid, I'm not inclined to rush. I stare at the wall and conjure up an image of the guard. Not one of her the last time I saw her when I was saving her ass, but one that's reminiscent of the many times I'd watched her interact with the inmates, treat them with respect and kindness. She'd been the only guard to actually give a fuck about any of us and look where that had gotten her.

As it always does when I think about her, my dick hardens. I ignore it, same as every other time. It feels wrong to be turned on by her, especially when I remember what almost happened to her. I shut off the water with my foot and fling the shower curtain open to grab a towel. I make quick work of drying off and getting dressed, not bothering to shave.

Back in the small room, I snatch my cell phone and wallet

off the nightstand. I leave the motel and walk to the attorney's office, needing the fresh air. It's only a few blocks, and besides, I haven't had time to get my car back yet.

The office comes into view, and before I know it, the walk is over. A chime sounds as I pull the door open and step into the spacious lobby area.

"Good morning, how may I help you?" The woman behind the desk sits up straight and smiles.

I smile back, the action still feeling foreign. She stares at me, and I take a moment to stare back. She's beautiful, with her blonde hair and blue eyes, but even I know that's a line that can't be crossed. Not that I want to. I'm in no position to have a relationship, not so soon after the last two years. Besides, she's probably got a polo-shirt wearing douche bag to go home to.

"Sir?" Her head tilts and I realize that my mind has wandered.

"Oh, sorry." I take a step closer to the reception desk and rest my forearms on the top, my tattoos a stark contrast to the glossy finished oak. "I'm Jett Stover. I've got an appointment with Mr. Ryder."

The woman glances at the computer screen, and her fingers fly over the keys, a look of concentration on her face. When she looks up again, the smile returns, and she nods to a group of chairs behind me.

"Have a seat. He'll be with you shortly."

I nod my thanks and sit down. There are several paintings on the walls, all of which are ugly as hell and probably cost a small fortune. The floor is marble with gold flecks, and for a minute, I wonder if the gold is real. Probably. This is definitely a fancy office, and I'm way out of my comfort zone. I'm sure my parents felt right at home here.

A tingle runs down my spine, and I glance at the receptionist. She quickly lowers her head and her cheeks pinken. I shift in my seat, feeling uncomfortable with her scrutiny and my surroundings. A door to the right of her desk opens, and an elderly man walks out, turning briefly to shake another man's hand. The men talk for a few more seconds before the older of the two walks out the door.

"Mr. Ryder, your ten o'clock is here."

"Thank you, Tracy."

The man I now know is the attorney I'm meeting with walks toward me and sticks out his hand.

"Mr. Stover?"

I stand and shake his hand. "It's just Jett." My voice is gruff, so I clear my throat.

"Right, well," he indicates the door he stepped through earlier. "Let's step into my office so we can get down to business."

I enter ahead of him and look around, my anxiety ratcheting up a notch. Everywhere I look screams money. There's a framed diploma on the wall to my right. There are bookshelves lining the wall behind the ornate desk, every inch filled with old books, none of which look like the fun kind.

"Please, have a seat."

Mr. Ryder sits in the green leather chair, and I take the one in front of me, the black leather more comfortable than I thought possible.

"I appreciate you coming in today." He shuffles through some papers on his desk until he finds what he's looking for. He opens the file and scans the contents before peering at me over his wire-rimmed glasses. "Jett, as you know, your parents had wills drawn up years ago, after the death of your brother."

"I didn't know that. I didn't know anything about a will until yesterday when you called me." I shift in my seat, anger heating my blood. My parents had been great at one time, but that was long ago, and I didn't want to think about how much they'd changed after we lost Harrison.

"Oh. Well, either way, I'm very sorry for your loss."

"Thanks. Can we cut the crap and get to why I'm here?" Mr. Ryder's eyes narrow at my callous words, but I don't give a damn. I lost my parents way before they actually died, and I don't want to rehash any of it, not with Mr. Ryder, not with anyone.

"I'll cut to the chase then." He grips a document and slides it across the desk toward me. "Your parents updated their wills just a few months before the accident. This is a list of the items remaining in the estate. It's not much, just a few heirlooms, but it's what they wanted kept for you. Everything is being held in a storage unit that has been paid for out of your inheritance."

I skim over the list and sigh. Fourteen items. That's what their lives have been reduced to. That's what I have left of my family.

"What about the money?" I know that sounds cold, but my savings won't last forever and I'm going to need the money more than I need the heirlooms. I'd rather have my family, but unless Mr. Ryder could bring people back from the dead, that isn't happening.

"The will stipulated that the money be held for you in a savings account until such time as you were released from prison. They had numerous investments and had done very well over the years. Some of their estate was donated to various charities and what remains is yours."

"Is that really what they thought?" I ask around clenched teeth.

"Excuse me?"

"That I was in prison? Is that really what they thought?"

"Ah, yes?" It comes out more like a question.

I huff out a hollow, humorless laugh and sit forward in

my chair. "Let's get one thing straight, Mr. Ryder." The attorney's eyes widen at the vehemence in my tone. "I'm a DEA agent and yes, I was in prison, but I was undercover. But *your clients* wouldn't know that because they never bothered to stay in touch with me."

"I'm, well, I'm sorry for the misunderstanding."

"It's more than a misunderstanding and not your apology to make." I lean back, the turn in the conversation mentally draining me.

"Mr. Stov—"

"Jett."

"Sorry… Jett," he corrects. "I must say, I confirmed the information they provided." Mr. Ryder shuffles through files on his desk, and when he finds what he's looking for, he hands it to me. "There's your arrest and prison record."

I skim through the papers in the folder and try to see what my parents saw. Granted, on paper, it looks bad. *I* look bad. The problem with that is the information is all made up as part of my cover. I slam the folder shut and toss it onto the desk.

"Undercover, Mr. Ryder. I was undercover. And that," I nod toward the discarded file. "That was my cover."

"I see. Well, I apologize for the—"

"Let's just get to the point. You called me here for a reason, right?" I look at him and ignore the censure that seeps into his eyes. He doesn't like me. Whatever. He doesn't have to. "How much?"

Mr. Ryder clears his throat. "Eleven million went to the aforementioned charities, and two point three million belongs to you."

My head snaps up, and I swallow down the laughter that's threatening to escape. Holy fuck! I was hoping there'd be enough to allow me to purchase a home rather than rent and maybe upgrade my vehicle. I never dreamed it would be that much. Before I can get too excited, I remind myself that my parents were assholes.

"What's the catch?" I ask, knowing there has to be one.

"Catch?" Mr. Ryder quirks an eyebrow and pushes his glasses up his nose.

"Yeah. There's no way they left me that kind of money without a few stipulations."

He looks through the papers in the file and returns his gaze to me. "There is one stipulation." He clears his throat. "The money is yours as long as you have no further legal problems. It states here that if you so much as get a speeding ticket, you forfeit what remains at that time."

"That sounds about right." I heave a sigh. "Whatever. We both know that's not going to be a problem."

"They just wanted what's best for you."

I huff out a chuckle at him. "Right. That's why they ignored me from the time I was ten and never bothered to learn who I *really* am as an adult. They should have won a medal for the world's best parents."

"Jett, believe what you will, but when they were here, they had nothing but good things to say about you."

"I doubt that."

"Sure, they were disappointed in your choices, but what parent isn't disappointed in their children at one point or another?" His gaze lands on a photo of what I presume to be his family. I choose to ignore the fact that he continues to talk as if my parents were right about me being a criminal. Clearly, it doesn't matter what I say. "I got to know them over the years. I considered them friends more than clients. And once a year, when they'd come in and update their wills, they'd sit right where you're sitting, and the entire time, they talked about you. And Harrison."

"Listen, I'm not up for a trip down memory lane. Just tell me what I need to do next."

Mr. Ryder sighs and slides another document toward me, along with a pen. "Sign that and you're good to go." He points to the 'X' at the bottom of the paper.

I sign where he indicates and stand up, indicating that I'm done. I want out of this stuffy office and away from the disapproving jackass in front of me. Mr. Ryder stands and hands me a large manilla envelope.

"Everything you need is in there, along with a key to the storage unit. If you have any questions, feel free to call me."

I take the thick envelope, thank him and walk out, not acknowledging the receptionist's 'Have a good day'. Outside the office, I let my neck roll and my head fall back. The sun is shining, and the chill is gone from the air. The packet in my hands is demanding my focus so I turn to the left and walk to the park where I can go through it and not worry about noisy motel guests.

The contents include the banking information, the address to the storage unit, as well as the number, and a letter from my parents. I don't read the letter, and while I itch to toss it in the trash, I don't. Maybe someday I'll give a shit about what they have to say, but today is not that day.

Once I'm satisfied that I have a plan, I go to the bank and withdraw a few hundred thousand, which causes the bank teller and manager to squirm, clearly not used to their customers leaving the premises with that much cash in hand.

As I leave the bank, I think about what to do next. I should head to the office, get some paperwork finished and cleared from my desk, but the thought of going back makes my stomach flip. Being a DEA agent is all I can ever remember wanting to be, but two years in prison, pretending to be someone I'm not has made me into someone I don't recognize.

When I'm back at the motel, I realize what I have to do. What I *want* to do. I pack up my shit and check out of my temporary housing and toss my bag over my shoulder. I call an Uber and have them drive me to the storage unit where my car has been stored.

After checking all of the fluids, I determine that the car will get me to where I need to go and I drive to a car lot on the other side of the city. I'm immediately drawn to a 1967 Chevy Impala. It's black, with chrome wheels, and worth every penny they're asking for it. I may have the money now, but with my vehicle as trade and my haggling ability, I manage to get them down a few grand.

I run a few more errands and make several phone calls before finding myself exactly where I said I didn't want to be: my office. Taking in my surroundings, I make my way to SAC Bing's office and when I arrive, I see that he's on the phone. He points to the chair across from his desk, and I take a seat.

While Bing continues his phone call, I force myself to relax and think about what I'm doing. I evaluate my motives and take stock of my meager plan, or more accurately, my lack of any type of plan.

I'm so lost in my own head that I'm startled when SAC Bing speaks.

"Jett, what brings you here? You're not due back for another two weeks."

For a moment, I second-guess myself. For a moment, I doubt that I'm in the right frame of mind to make such a big decision. For a moment, I—

"Jett?"

My gaze meets my boss's and just like that, the moment and all the self-doubt vanish. A sense of clarity washes over me, and I'm more confident in my decision than anything else I've ever done in my life.

"I quit."

3

EMMA

A year and a half later...

The credits roll on the television, and I swipe at the tears on my cheeks. I've watched *A Star is Born* a dozen times, and it never seems to matter that I know what's going to happen. It still makes me ugly cry.

I throw my blanket off of me and grab the empty bowl on the coffee table as I stand. I ate a few scoops of mint chocolate chip ice cream earlier, and though I want more, I resist the temptation. As I start the dishwasher, the sound of an engine floats through the open kitchen window over the sink.

I look out at the headlights shining against the garage next door and frown. That house has been empty since before I moved in a year ago. From what the realtor told me, the elderly couple that lived there moved to Florida to enjoy their retirement. The rest of the block is lined with houses, some with couples and some with families.

The street is quiet, despite several younger children and that's what drew me to it. After the riot, I tried to stay where I was, but PTSD sank its hooks into me and wouldn't let go. The only option was to move across town and pray that the change in scenery would help. I wanted to move out of the state, but my family is here and so is my best friend, Sierra.

When I look back through the screen, the headlights are gone, but I catch sight of the vehicle with its doors and trunk open. I watch as a man carries boxes from the car into the house and duck down when his head swivels my way. The action reminds me just how crazy I've become over the last year and a half, and I force myself to stand. I reach up and pull the window down, flip the latch and draw the curtains closed. It's too dark for me to really see anything anyway so no point in keeping them open.

Yeah, keep telling yourself that.

I turn to head back to the living room and put in another movie. My anxiety is high tonight, and I pull my cell phone from my sweat's pocket, not bothering to even hit 'play' on the remote. I put the device to my ear and smile when the ringback tone comes over the line.

"Hey, girl," Sierra answers on what sounds like a yawn.

"Hey. What're you doin'?" I ask the question, even though I know I woke her up.

"Nothin'."

It's the same every time I call this late. Sierra is a kindergarten teacher and has to be up early, but she never ignores my calls. Never.

"I can let you go back to—"

"Stop it. You called for a reason. What's up?" The sound of rustling sheets comes through the line. She's making herself comfortable, knowing this is likely to be a long call. I have no idea why she puts up with me, but I know I won the freaking lottery in the best friend department.

"I have a new neighbor," I blurt out. Shame floods my system because this news is not something a normal person would need to share at nearly midnight, but for me, it's huge.

"Oh yeah? Is he cute?"

"How do you know it's a man?"

"Honey, if it were a woman, you wouldn't be calling me." There's no judgment in her tone though I know there should be. I'm judging myself nine ways to hell so why wouldn't she?

"That's not true," I argue, the lie evident even to *my* ears.

"It is true, but it's okay." She sighs. "Em, it's okay to be something other than scared. You know that, right?"

"It's been almost two years! I should be over it by now."

"PTSD hits people differently. You know this. I know that the incident was traumatic, and I'm not saying that you should pretend it didn't happen, but you have to start living." She never calls it what it was: a prison riot, near-rape, assault. It's always 'the incident'. "Maybe having a new neighbor is a good place to start."

"I'm living," I protest.

"You're alive, yes, but going to the grocery store to pick up your online order is not living. Doing all your shopping on Amazon is not living. Staying home and burying yourself in your fear is not living." I hear a rustling sound like she's switching her phone to the other ear. "When was the last time you went anywhere that wasn't absolutely necessary?"

I don't want to answer that question. Mostly because it makes me sound pathetic. I used to have friends, go out for drinks with them, go shopping. Now most would categorize me as a recluse, a loser. Everyone but Sierra and my parents and brother have long since forgotten about me. After a few months of me trying to maintain my life, my habits, and always ending up in a panic, my circle of friends disappeared, one by one. Even Len, the prison doctor that always pestered me for dates quit calling.

"That's what I thought."

"I can't have a life. You know that. I tried and it didn't work. I'm too damaged." My throat closes up and tears threaten to spill over my lashes.

"You can, Em. And you're not damaged. You had a bad experience, and it changed things for you. But hasn't it taken enough from you? Do you really want to give it the rest of your life?"

"I don't know."

"You're stubborn, you know that?" She chuckles, reminding me of why I love her so much. She isn't afraid to say what she's thinking, and she hasn't let any of my insecurities push her away. "I have an idea."

"What?" I ask, hesitantly. If there's one thing I know for certain, it's not going to be something I'll like.

"In the morning, go over and introduce yourself to your new neighbor. That's it. Just a friendly 'hello'. You don't have to have a conversation or even exchange more than a few words, but maybe you'll surprise yourself."

"I don't think th—"

"Don't think, just do. It won't be so bad, I guarantee it."

"Yeah, maybe."

"Promise me you'll do it?"

"We'll see."

A giant sigh escapes her. "Okay. I guess that'll have to be good enough."

"You should get back to bed. I'm sorry I woke you up."

"You know you can call me any time, day or night. I'm always here for you."

"I know. And thanks. You're the best."

"I am, aren't I?" She laughs and just like that, the tension of the conversation is gone. "Get some sleep, Em. Everything always looks better in the morning."

"So you say. Love you."

"Ditto. 'Night Em."

Sierra disconnects the call, and I drop my phone into my lap. I think about what she suggested and all that does is make my stomach clench and beads of sweat pool at the base of my spine. I don't know why I'm so scared of introducing myself, and when I go to bed, I've convinced myself that I'm not afraid and that I *will* go next door, first thing in the morning.

My sleep is filled with nightmares, like it is most nights, and when, at four in the morning, I give up on getting a restful night's sleep, I flip on the bedside lamp and grab my Kindle lying next to it. I read until the sun comes up and then trudge to the shower to wash off the stink of fear-induced sweat.

While I'm in the shower, I give myself a pep-talk, still prepared to do what Sierra suggested. By the time I'm clean, dressed and standing in front of my stove flipping eggs, my PTSD has won, and I know I'm not going to follow through. I eat my breakfast, chastising myself the entire time, and when I'm done, I carry my dishes to the sink. I wash them by hand, too lazy to unload the dishwasher, and when I hear the sound of a power tool, I push aside one curtain panel with a wet, soapy hand.

My new neighbor is standing in his backyard and cutting wood into long planks. I briefly wonder what he's making but then realize it doesn't matter. It's not like I can ask him so why even speculate? Just as I convince myself that I don't care, I catch sight of his raised arm swiping at his forehead.

Tattoos peek out from beneath pushed up long sleeves, and muscles bunch under the white cotton. I let my gaze travel over the expanse of his broad shoulders, down his back to an ass encased in worn jeans. I swallow around the cotton balls in my mouth and am jerked out of my trance when water splashes up my arm.

I look down and notice that I dropped my plate into the sink, causing the dirty water to slosh over the sides and down the front of the cupboards. I let the curtain fall back into place and grab a towel to clean up my mess. As I'm kneeling on the floor to wipe down the cupboards, a thought occurs to me.

I may be damaged, but if my reaction to my new neighbor is any indication, I'm not dead.

4

JETT

I've been in my new house for a week, and I still wake up every morning wondering where the hell I am. I roll out of bed and trudge toward the bathroom attached to the master bedroom. I take in the tiled shower stall, large whirlpool tub, and double sinks. I don't need this much room, but the craftsman style home appeals to me. Not to mention the fact that it sits on a cul-de-sac and has no signs of the seedier side of life I've become used to.

I could have gotten a larger home, more land, but when the realtor showed me this listing, I wanted it immediately. I paid cash which means no mortgage payment which in turn means I can take a little more time before I find a job. Quitting the DEA was a smart decision, but after traveling around the country for so long, I'm ready to put down roots.

I want to work, I really do, but I also want to finish the few projects to make this house exactly what I want. The first project has been a fence for the backyard so I can get a dog. One thing I learned during my travels, is that I don't particularly like being alone. A dog will help with that.

As the hot water sluices over my body, I think back over

the dream I had the night before. It was of the guard, again, only this time it didn't end the same as reality. Last night it ended with her in my arms, in my bed, after a particularly satisfying orgasm delivered by yours truly.

The image in my mind has my dick springing to life, and I fist myself. I brace myself against the cool tile and close my eyes. I've resisted this temptation for so long but not today. I can't quite get the right rhythm so I lather up some soap and return to my fantasy. As my hand glides up and down my cock, the suds providing the feeling I'm going for, I let my mind convince me it's her mouth and not my hand. I've jacked off many times in my life, even had several one-night stands since leaving the DEA, but something about the build up of this orgasm feels different. Maybe because it's the first time I've let myself think of *her* while doing it.

My spine tingles and my balls draw uptight. I increase my speed and tighten my grip. Cum spurts out of me and onto the wall. When I'm done, my legs are shaking and it takes me a minute to return to Earth. If it feels that good on my own, I can only imagine what the real thing would feel like. Not that I'd ever get the chance to find out. Not with her.

I wash my hair, the shaggy strands reminding me that I need to get a haircut. When I'm done, I reach out to the heated towel rack and pluck off the thick terry cloth and dry off. I throw on a pair of running shorts, a T-shirt and my tennis shoes. Before I get started on the last of my fence, I'll get in a quick run and workout.

My feet hit the pavement as I jog down the street, nodding to those I pass and wondering if they're always this friendly. Probably not. In my experience, nothing is ever as it seems. I get in five miles and when I return to the house, I head straight to the basement where I've set up some equipment. Nothing much, just a punching bag, weight bench, and treadmill.

I spend the next hour going through my routine, and after rehydrating, I head out back to finish up the fence. I'm not working for ten minutes when the sensation of being watched comes over me. It's the same as every other time. I'm certain that this is a great place to live, but it seems I have a very nosy neighbor.

I glance over my shoulder towards the little house that needs a lot of work and smile when the curtain falls back into place. I have yet to meet the person behind the window but want to. They must be lonely if all they do is watch me. I assume it's an older individual, but I have no idea if they're male or female. They haven't so much as stepped onto the porch since I moved in. I really should get over there and introduce myself, but since they haven't done it first, I figure it can wait.

I return my attention back to my table saw and finish making the last cut needed. Another four hours and the fence is complete. I stand on the back porch and survey my handiwork. Not too bad for a guy with no background in construction. Now that the backyard is secure, I clean up my mess and take another quick shower to rinse off the grime of working hard. I want to go to the animal shelter and pick out my new buddy.

As I back out of the driveway, something catches my eye. I glance towards the neighbor's house and see a pair of eyes looking out a side window. When I wave, the curtain shifts back into place. I chuckle and shake my head, letting my gaze drop to the overgrown flower beds by their front porch. I make a mental note to get some mulch and flowers while I'm out. Maybe if I help out a little, that'll coax them out.

I run some errands to get supplies for a dog, and for the flower beds, before going to the animal shelter. Once there, I quickly realize that I may be in over my head. Every cage I come to has a sad-looking dog that stares at me and silently begs me to choose them. I know I can't get more than one, at least not right away, and I end up taking home a beautiful white boxer that the shelter owner says was surrendered by its owner when they realized she was deaf. She's not even a year old and will need lots of training, but her little nub twitched back and forth so fast and I found I couldn't walk away from her.

On the drive home, I put the window down and laugh when she sticks her head out and her jowls blow back and slobber flies from her face. It looks like she's smiling, and I can't help but understand what she's experiencing. Freedom from the cage, freedom from feeling unwanted and unloved. It's a heady feeling, and I vow to make sure she never feels anything but good for the rest of her life.

When I pull back into my driveway, I unload the car and try to think of a name for the dog. The only name that comes to mind is Freedom so that's what I settle on.

"Hey, Freedom. C'mon girl."

I open the passenger door and pat my leg to coax her out. I know she can't hear me, but that doesn't stop me from talking to her. She hops down and I secure the leash I bought and walk her through the gate and into the backyard. After letting her loose, I stand back and watch her run in circles, happy in her new home.

I decide to tackle the mulch job next door and let Freedom play in the yard. I lug the mulch next to my car to the front of the neighbor's house. I start pulling weeds, and it doesn't take as long as I thought. I stand up and lift my shirt to wipe the sweat from my face. Before I have a chance to work on planting the flowers, a car pulls into the driveway, and I'm startled to see it's a young woman, maybe in her thirties.

She sees me and frowns, no doubt wondering what the hell I'm doing. I know this isn't the owner of the house because whoever the hell that is has been peeking through the curtains the entire time I've been working. Maybe it's their granddaughter.

I walk toward her and reach out my hand to shake hers.

"Hi. I'm Jett."

She looks at my hand but doesn't shake it. I drop it back to my side and smile. I know I'm probably overstepping, but she doesn't have to look at me like that. I'm doing her family a favor after all.

"I live next door." I point to my house over her shoulder. Her eyes grow comically round, and I wonder what she's thinking. "I was just trying to help out. I hope your grandparents don't mind."

"My grandparents?" Her brows raise.

"Yeah." I nod to the house I'm standing in front of. "They've been watching me work ever since I moved in."

"Wait, you think my grandparents live here?" she asks.

"Well, yeah. I mean, it's the only thing that makes sense. Why else would they never leave the house? I figure whoever it is, they're elderly and just don't get out much."

The corners of her eyes crinkle, and her lips pinch. After a second, she starts laughing, no longer bothering to control it. I narrow my eyes at her and shift from one foot to the other.

"What's so funny?"

She sobers for a moment before losing it again. Tears are streaming down her cheeks, and while I'm glad she finds me so entertaining, I'm starting to get annoyed. I cross my arms over my chest and brace my feet apart.

"I'm sorry." She waves a hand in front of her face and manages to stop laughing. "It's just, oh man, I needed that."

I relax my stance and let my arms fall to my sides, but I don't speak.

"My grandparents don't live here. In fact, they're dead." She looks me up and down, a smile spreading across her face.

"I'm sorry to hear that."

Again, that hand flaps, waving away my condolences. "It was years ago. They were old. It happens."

Not really sure what to say to that, I settle on, "So, your parents then?"

"What? No, not my parents." She braces a hand on a cocked hip. "I'm guessing she hasn't introduced herself. I tried to tell her she should, that it wasn't going to be hard. Maybe if she had, she'd realize what a hotty she's got for a neighbor."

"Who?" I'm having a hard time following her train of thought. "Are we still talking about whoever lives here?"

"Yes." She heaves a dramatic sigh, apparently frustrated with my lack of understanding. "My friend lives here. My *best* friend."

"Oh."

"She called me the night you moved in, and I told her she should introduce herself to you."

"I see."

"I'm guessing by your confusion that she hasn't done that."

"Uh, no, she hasn't."

"But you said she's been watching you?"

"I've seen someone peeking through the curtains. Maybe she wasn't watching me." I shrug, clearly having misread the entire situation.

"Oh, I have no doubt she was watching you." She winks.

"Okay. Maybe you can introduce me?" Maybe the friend is disabled in some way. Why else would she just watch me through the window and never come out?

"I'd love to, but…" She pulls her bottom lip between her teeth, worry passing over her eyes.

"But what?"

"She's had a rough couple of years." When my eyebrows furrow, she rushes to add, "She's great, really, but something happened, and she's never been the same."

"That sucks." I know what that's like. To feel like you have it all and then it's gone in a flash.

"It does. I've known her since grade school, and she—" Her cell phone rings and she reaches into her purse to get it. When she looks at the screen, she frowns but answers it. "Hey. Yeah, I'm here. Oh, well then come outside. C'mon, Em." Based on her side of the conversation, I assume she's talking to her friend who is just a few feet away in the house. She sighs. "Okay, fine. I'll be in in a minute. I won't, I promise." She ends the call and drops the device back in her bag. "Sorry 'bout that."

"No problem. Everything okay?"

"Yeah, it's fine. She's just worried I'll tell you all her secrets." I can't tell if she's joking or not, so I don't speak. "I better go. It was nice to meet you."

"You too." As she turns and starts up the stairs, I call out to her. "I never did catch your name."

"Sierra," she calls over her shoulder.

I watch as she stands there and twists the knob, finding it locked. I hear a few deadbolts click, and the door swings open.

I suck in a breath when I see who my neighbor is. It's Emma, the guard I saved, the guard from my dreams.

Fucking hell.

5

EMMA

"What's wrong? You look like you've seen a ghost."

Sierra's hand is on my arm and her voice is full of concern, but I can't get my feet to move. I'm rooted to the spot and staring at my closed door, willing the man in my front yard to go away.

"Em, talk to me." Sierra shakes me, pulling me out of the haze that's threatening to suffocate me. "What the hell's going on?"

"That's him," I manage to push out.

"Who?"

I point to the door like that answers her question. She follows my finger, and her brows knit together.

"Your neighbor?"

I nod and swallow past the lump in my throat. "How did I miss that?"

"Miss what?"

"Do you have any idea who that is?" I'm suddenly able to move, and I stalk toward the couch and throw myself down, grabbing a throw pillow and hugging it to my chest like a child.

"He said his name's Jett." She plops down beside me. "And get this… he thought you were my grandparents." She's laughing but all I manage is a groan. When she realizes that I'm not seeing the humor, she sobers. "What's wrong?"

"That's him. That's Storm." I look her in the eyes and watch as she tries to put the puzzle pieces together. I know the second she does because her eyes light up and her mouth forms an 'O'.

"Wait. *That's* Storm? As in the hunky-inmate-who-saved-your-life, Storm?" She turns sideways so she's facing me and pulls a leg under her. When I nod, she says, "But he said his name is Jett."

"It is. That's his real name. His nickname in prison was Storm. I never knew his actual name until after he saved me." I chew on my bottom lip. "Why is he here?"

"I don't know. But he is." She reaches out and pulls one of my hands away from the pillow and squeezes it. "Maybe this isn't such a bad thing."

"How is this not a bad thing?" I snap. "I already can't face the world. Now I have to have a daily reminder of the worst day of my life." I pull out of her grasp and stand to pace. "I have to move. I have to call the realtor and find ano—"

"Em, stop." Sierra grips my shoulders and stops me from wearing a hole into the hardwood floor. "You are not calling a realtor. You are not moving. You can't keep running from this."

"You don't get it."

"You're right. I don't. But I do get you. And this isn't who you are. At least, it's not who you were."

"People change."

"Sure they do. And it's not always a bad thing. But seriously, Em, do you like who you've changed into?"

I let my head fall so I don't have to see the look in her eyes.

"Em, listen to me." She cups my cheeks and forces me to raise my head. "You listening?"

"I'm listening," I mumble.

"Maybe having Storm, or Jett, or whatever you want to call him, so close is a good thing. He saved you. He wasn't the bad guy that day." Her lips curve into a sad smile. "Maybe, just *maybe*, he's the one person who knows what happened and can help you through it."

I hear what she's saying, and it makes sense, but every fiber of my being wants to deny it. Every part of me wants to run fast and run far. A thud on the porch pulls my attention away from Sierra.

"What was that?" I ask as I step away from her and toward the window.

"He was fixing up your flower beds when I got here." I look over my shoulder at her in time to see her shrug. "My guess is he's just finishing up."

I pull the curtain aside and see a bag of mulch on the porch. That must have been what I heard. I watch as he walks across my driveway and down his own toward his back yard. He's probably checking on the dog I saw him bring home.

"He said you've been watching him."

My head snaps up at her words.

"It's okay if you have been." She takes a tentative step toward me. "But maybe you should ask yourself why you've been watching him." The tilt of her head is all too familiar. She always does it when she really wants to drive home her point. Right now, it's annoying as hell.

"Fine. I've been watching him. But just because he's been making so much damn noise with his sawing and drilling and hammering."

"Uh-huh."

"Seriously, he's been an awful neighbor so far. He's loud and frustrating and doesn't know the meaning of sleeping in."

"And he's sexy as sin. And kind. And he planted you flowers." Her smile is mocking, and I itch to smack it off of her. Not that I ever would. "I just have one question."

"What?"

"How did you *not* know it was him? I mean, if you have been watching him," she holds her hand up when I open my mouth to speak. "I'm not judging, just stating a fact. If you've been watching him, how did you not know?"

I shrug. "I never saw his face. He's always got his back turned toward my place when he's working in the backyard. And then the fence was in the way."

"Makes sense, I guess."

"Look, can we quit talking about him? Please?" I walk to the kitchen and pull out the wine and wine glasses.

"Of course," she says as she follows me.

I pour us both a glass of red wine, and we carry them to the couch. Sierra's here for our weekly movie night and somehow, it's been a rough start.

You freaked the fuck out. That's more than just a rough start.

"What're we watching tonight?" she asks, pulling me from my internal chastising.

"It's your turn to pick."

I hand her the remote, and she turns on Netflix. She scrolls through a few movies before she settles on a chick flick. By the time the movie is over, we've killed the bottle of wine and started on another. This is a regular occurrence with us, which is why Sierra keeps clothes at my place, in case she needs to spend the night.

"That was so good," she says on her way to the kitchen to open a second bottle.

"Yep."

She comes back with the open bottle and looks at me. "You have no idea what it was even about, do you?"

I realize she's right. I watched the movie but was thinking about Jett the entire time. I'm not about to admit that though. "It was a rom-com. Girl meets guy. Girl falls in love with guy. Guy pulls a dick move. Girl forgives him. Happily ever after."

"That's every chick flick ever made. Not too hard to figure out." She takes a sip of her wine and eyes me. "You were thinking about *him*, weren't you?"

"No."

"Right. You keep telling yourself that."

"You getting hungry?" I ask, hoping to change the subject and also remembering that I haven't eaten since lunch.

"Starved. I picked the movie, you pick the food." That's our deal. We swap duties every week to keep it fair.

"How about Chinese?"

"Sounds good to me. I'd say we could go pick it up but neither of us should probably drive."

"I'll call and have it delivered."

While we wait for our dinner, we both change into pajamas and figure out what we're going to watch next. When the food arrives thirty minutes later, Sierra pays the delivery driver, like she always does, so I don't have to answer the door to a stranger. We divvy up the contents of our order and resettle on the couch.

Two movies later and stuffed full of Chinese food, ice cream and wine, Sierra is passed out on the couch. I cover her with a blanket and start to turn off the lights throughout the house. When I reach the one above the sink, I notice a light on next door and look out. Jett is outside with the dog. He's sitting on his back step, and the dog is running around like it's never been able to before. I watch for a few minutes before flipping the switch and bathing the room in darkness.

I usually leave it on, but with Sierra here, I don't mind having it off.

I use my cell phone's flashlight to walk back through the house and up to my bedroom. Once there, I crawl into bed and stare at the ceiling for a long time, my thoughts swirling with unanswered questions.

Why is Jett here?

When was he released?

Does he know I'm his neighbor?

What if him being here makes my PTSD worse?

I force myself to close my eyes and do the deep breathing techniques my trauma therapist taught me. I hate going to bed because that's when the nightmares come so it's usually a process. Eventually, the techniques work and sleep sucks me in.

6

JETT

"Hey man, what's up?"

I was in the backyard, playing fetch with Freedom, when my phone rang.

"It's been a while. Figured I'd give you time to settle in before bugging the shit outta you for an invite to watch a game or something," Slade says.

Slade and I haven't talked more than a few times since I left the DEA. He and Jackson have been keeping me updated on the Jeffrey Lee case, and I appreciate it. Lee is dangerous and who knows if he'll ever be a threat to me. I can handle myself, but it's nice to know I have others I can count on too.

"Didn't know you wanted an invite." I toss the ball to Freedom and go sit on one of the patio chairs I bought for the back deck.

"And now you do. You busy later? I can pick up some beers and steaks and we can hang out."

"Sounds good." A car door catches my attention, and I rush to the fence in time to see Emma backing out of her driveway. So she does leave the house.

It's been a week since I met her friend, Sierra, and since I realized that she's my mysterious neighbor. Every once in a while I still catch her watching me, but I've yet to talk to her. Sierra mentioned a 'bad history' and I know exactly what she was talking about. I don't want to scare Emma and figure she'll talk to me if and when she's ready.

"Jett, are you even listening?"

"Huh? Oh, yeah."

"You got a girl over or something?"

I glance at Freedom. "As a matter of fact."

"Seriously? And you answered the phone?"

I laugh at the incredulity in his tone. "She doesn't mind."

"What kind of woman doesn't mind interruptions? Brandie would start throwing shit at my head."

"The kind with four legs, fur and a tail."

"You got a dog?"

"Yeah. Little white boxer, Freedom. Cute as hell and a shitton of energy."

"I bet. I'll let you get back to her then. See ya later."

"I'll be here."

I disconnect the call as Freedom drops her ball in my lap. I play fetch with her for another hour or so, until I hear Emma's car pull into her driveway. I go to the gate but stop myself from opening it. I want to talk to her, explain to her that I didn't know she lived here. I don't know if she even cares, but the fact that she has yet to say 'hi' speaks volumes.

Or maybe she just doesn't like you because she thinks you're a felon.

I discard that thought quickly as I remember the way she was with the prisoners. She was never one to judge, so I really don't think that's the problem. Besides, wouldn't they have told her who I really was after the riot?

Another car door slamming catches my attention, and I look through the gate to see Slade walking toward the front of the house. I unhook the latch and call out to him, forcing myself to not look in Emma's direction.

Slade switches direction and waves as he strolls to where I'm standing.

"Nice place." He sets his bags down and pulls me in for a back-slapping hug. "Good to see you finally settling in and giving up the nomad lifestyle." He laughs at his wit and so do I. I catch sight of Emma over his shoulder and she's frowning, clearly having heard what Slade said.

"It was fun for a while, but it was time," I say as I pull away and usher him through the yard and into the house.

Freedom follows close behind, begging for attention. Slade obliges and gets slobbered on for it. The drool doesn't seem to bother him, which is good because I'm not about to scold her for just being a dog.

Slade and I forgo watching whatever game may be on TV and spend time talking about Lee.

"Any new leads?" I ask.

"That's actually why I wanted to come over," he responds, shifting in the dining room chair he's occupying. He tips his beer and takes a few swallows before continuing. "We've gone through all of the intel you obtained undercover, numerous times, and we think we found something."

"And you're just now bringing it up?" I quirk a brow at him.

"You're lucky I'm bringing it up at all," he snaps, unable to hide his frustration. "Look, Jackson and I shouldn't even be keeping you in the loop but..."

"But what?" I prod when the silence lingers a little too long.

"But," he draws the word out. "We both agree that you deserve to know what's going on after everything you've been through." He looks away and clears his throat. I never told them all of the shit that went down when I was undercover, but they aren't stupid. I quit my job so they have to know something other than the riot happened. "Anyway, we were able to use some of the information you obtained and find a digital trail of communication between Lee and who we assume is an interested buyer."

"Buyer?"

"Yeah. Seems he escaped and picked up right where he left off with the family business. We think the buyer has a specific girl in mind. From what we can tell, Lee doesn't have the girl yet, so we've got our cyber division working hard on trying to figure out locations, dates, specifics."

"Jesus."

"It's definitely not what we were hoping for when you went undercover, but no one could have predicted the riot. That fucked with the entire case."

"No kidding," I mumble. "It fucked with more than the case." I take a deep breath and hold it for a second before releasing the air. "So, any other good news?"

He laughs but without humor. "Nope, that's it." He glances around the open concept living space of my home. "Looks like you've got a lot going on here."

"Yeah," I respond and then launch into a litany about all of the projects I'm working on and want to complete to make the house more *me*. "How's Brandie doing?"

Slade's chest puffs out, and his mouth tilts into a grin. "She's great," he says proudly. He downs the rest of his beer and sets the bottle on the table. "Have you met anyone since moving in?"

"Nah." I catch myself before my eyes give me away by turning toward Emma's house.

"You really want me to believe that you've been here for what, a few weeks, and you haven't been to any local bars and found someone to pass the time with?" He stands and carries his empty bottle to the trash to drop it in.

"Don't know what to tell you." I shrug. "I've been busy."

"What about that chick I saw when I pulled up? She your neighbor?"

I nod before finishing my beer and grabbing another.

"And?" He drags the word out.

"And nothing. Just a neighbor."

"Jesus, I figured you'd have someone warming your bed pretty quick. You found plenty of chicks to bang on the road. What, the neighbor not good enough for you or something?"

I'm out of my chair so fast it crashes to the floor. I grab Slade by his shirt and lift him until his toes barely touch the hardwood.

"Watch your fucking mouth. Emma's way too good for me."

He quirks a brow, and I realize my reaction gave me away. I shove him away from me, and he stumbles but catches himself before he falls.

"Just a neighbor, huh?"

"Shut up." I right my chair and straddle it, letting my forearms rest on the back.

"No. Tell me about her."

I don't remember Slade being such a childish asshole. Maybe he's just trying to vicariously relive his single days through me now that he's married with a baby on the way.

"Not much to tell. At least, not more than you already know." He knows about the riot and what almost happened to the guard. He knows her name, how I saved her.

When he doesn't put two and two together, I throw him a bone. "She's the guard."

His eyes grow round and he whistles. "That's some heavy shit. She's *the* Emma?"

"One and the same."

"What's it been like with her now that she knows who you really are?"

"Hasn't been like anything. I haven't talked to her." I stand and grab the steaks, needing to do something, anything to keep my body occupied. It has a tendency to react to the thought of her, and I do *not* need Slade seeing that shit.

"What do you mean you haven't talked to her? I thought for sure you would have at least reached out to check on her, make sure she's okay." He pauses and his eyes narrow. "Wait. That's why you finally decided to settle in one place isn't it? Because you *did* track her down… to here."

"Not true. Didn't even know she lived here until a week after I moved in."

"So it's just a coincidence that she's your next-door neighbor? That she's within spitting distance of you? I call bullshit."

"You can call bullshit all you want, but it's true. I had no idea. Not until I met a friend of hers outside one day." I didn't mention that it was when I was fixing Emma's flower beds. He'd jump all over that.

"Wow." He scratches his chin and stands next to the grill as I fire it up to cook the steaks. "What's the hold-up then?"

"Her friend said that she went through something that changed her. I know she was talking about the riot, and I figure if Emma wants to talk to me, she will. It's more likely that she wants nothing to do with me because I'll remind her of it all. I don't want to do that to her."

"I get that, man, but she's, like, I don't know. '*It* for you' is the best way I know how to say it. She got her hooks in you that day, whether she meant to or not, and you've never bothered to remove them."

I whirl on him. "I was a man in prison who hadn't felt a woman in two years. Of course, I held on to the idea of her. But that's all it was and all it will ever be… an idea. Let it go."

"But—"

"Let. It. Go."

He backs away with his hands up in surrender. "Fine."

The rest of the evening is tense, but we move past the whole Emma conversation. We even find better topics than Jeffrey Lee. When he takes off around midnight, I realize that Slade and I could be friends. Good friends. If he can get it out of his head that Emma is 'the one' for me.

When I take Freedom out for her last run of the night, I notice that Emma's house is still lit up like a Christmas tree. I stand there, watching for the tell-tale sign of the curtain moving but see nothing. Freedom runs to the door, and I give up and go inside, giving the dog her treat.

I snag the last beer and plop on the couch, recounting my conversation with Slade. What he said about Emma getting her hooks into me is true, but I know she didn't mean to. Not only that, but what kind of dick does it make me that it happened at a time when she was at her most vulnerable? The worst kind, that's what.

During the riot, I didn't want to get involved. I didn't want to jeopardize two years of hard work and sacrifice. Lee was not the easy target I was led to believe he would be. He was a crazy fucker, and not many of the guys would dare to cross him. Most would bend to his will and ended up his bitch. I managed to get close to him and gain his trust, but that all came to a screeching halt the night of the riot.

I was able to sit back and keep my mouth shut until he pushed Emma to the floor. It was hard to watch as he smacked her around, but at least that would only cause bruises and those heal. If I let him rape her, that was a level of evil I feared she'd never recover from. So I stepped in, stopped him. Up until that point, she had spunk, a fighting spirit about her, but at that moment, it failed her.

When I lifted her up and covered her with the blanket, I asked her to trust me, I wasn't too hopeful that she would listen. But she surprised me. When she was in my arms, I was able to pretend, just for a moment, that she was meant to be there, that I was carrying her to a comfy bed where I lay her out and worship her body. The moment passed and I remembered that I was a prisoner to her, one she was tasked to keep in line. Two years locked up with murderers and rapists had warped my mind in a way that I'm still recovering from.

I carried her, sure. I even laid her out before me. But it was on rock hard pavement with guns pointed at my head and SWAT yelling at me. Not exactly romantic. Even if it was all for show.

Sitting on my couch, remembering the way she felt against me, her bare skin under my fingertips, has my dick hardening and begging to be freed. Disgusted with myself for getting turned on thinking about what was likely the worst day of her life, I down the remainder of my beer and head straight to the bathroom.

I turn on the shower and strip out of my clothes. I step under the cold spray, letting it cool my lust. I manage to dampen it, barely, before crawling into bed. I don't bother with clothes, and when the sheets brush my skin, my cock jumps back to life.

I give up the fight and take myself in hand, trying to conjure up images of other women, any other woman. I fail miserably. I jerk off to an image of Emma, bent over a table, ass sticking out for me. I growl out my release and roll out of bed to see Freedom standing there, tongue lolling out of her mouth, silently judging me for what I just did. I turn away from her, strip the sheets from the bed and go back to the shower to wash off.

Back in bed, Freedom lying next to me, I give in to the inevitability that I'm going to have to talk to Emma at some point. I think about how to make that happen without her feeling threatened or pressured to interact with me, and when I have a plan, I give in to sleep.

∼

Something pulls me from my dream, and I bolt upright, straining to listen to the sounds of the night, trying to figure out what woke me. That's when I hear it. A scream.

Whoever it is, they sound terrified and my first thought is of my pretty neighbor. I throw off the covers and am grateful that I put shorts on after my second shower. I hear the scream again, and it's louder this time. I grab my gun out of the nightstand and then take off down the stairs and out the front door. There's another scream, and I'm able to determine that it *is* coming from Emma's house.

Light still streams through her windows, but I can't tell what's going on. All I know is that she's screaming like she's dying so something bad is going down. I ram my shoulder into her front door and don't give a second thought to the fact that it was locked. The door crashes into the wall, and I shoot up her stairs, following the sounds of terror.

I find her bedroom door, and when I throw it open, gun aimed at an invisible monster, I freeze.

Emma is in bed, twisted in sheets that appear to be soaked through with sweat. And she's alone. Her head thrashes from side to side, and she's mumbling incoherently between her screams. I stand there, trying to determine if I should wake her up or go back home. I remember the busted front door and decide against leaving. Besides, she shouldn't have to experience whatever the hell she's experiencing.

I tuck my weapon into the waistband of my shorts. I walk to the bed and try to capture her flailing arms. It's not easy, but I manage to pin them down. She still doesn't wake up, so I sit down next to her.

"Emma, wake up." I talk quietly but firmly. "Emma, it's Jett. C'mon, doll. You're safe. Wake up for me."

Emma's body begins to relax as my voice penetrates the mental torture, and her eyes slowly open. When she sees me, her eyes widen in fear, and she yanks away to scramble up the bed. She'd melt into the headboard if she could.

"Why the fuck are you in my bedroom?"

I stand up and back away so she can see I'm no threat to her. "I heard you scream. I thought something was wrong, and I came to make sure you were okay. That's it."

She looks around the room, seemingly to measure the truth of my words, and when she finds no one else there, she pulls her knees to her chest and drops her head. I hear what sounds like sniffling, and when her shoulders start to jerk, I know she's crying. Sobbing.

"Aw, doll, what's wrong?" I go to her, no longer worried about appearing like a threat.

When I sit next to her and slide my arm around her shoulders, she stiffens but doesn't pull away. The scent of vanilla is strong, and it's mixed with a hint of fear. I recognize the smell from the night of the riot. She smelled exactly the same then. I breathe in through my nose, wanting to intoxicate myself with it. I rest my cheek against her hair, not caring that it's matted with sweat.

"Emma, don't cry. It was just a dream. You're fine. I promise you're safe." I hold her tighter, as tight as she'll let me, offering her whatever comfort she needs.

"It, it, it's not, just, a, a, a dream," she stutters through her sobs. "It, it, it happened," she wails.

I pull my arm from around her and shuffle to sit in front of her. I cup her cheeks with my hands and force her to look at me. She tries to resist, but I'm much stronger. When she gives up the fight and her luminous blue eyes lock onto mine, my heart cracks at the sadness, the fear. Her nose is red and runny, and I've still never seen a woman half as beautiful as her.

"Emma, this time, it *was* just a dream." She has to have been dreaming of that night, the riot. I can't imagine anything else that would do this to her. "Do you remember me?"

She nods and rubs her nose with the back of her hand.

"Good. I don't want to scare you, but I also don't want to leave until I know you're okay. I need you to tell me what you want me to do." I pray she doesn't tell me to make tracks, but I will if she does. I'd never hurt her. I think she knows that, but I'm not certain. "What do you want me to do?"

Her eyes dart around the room again and land on the bed. I don't move so much as a muscle.

"Can you, um, get me a glass of water? From the bathroom?"

She points to a door behind me, and I get up to get her what she wants. I find an empty glass on the bathroom counter and fill it with tap water. When I return to the room, she's standing up and trying to remove the sheets from the bed. I rush to her side and take them from her hand and give her the glass.

"Here, let me."

She downs the water, and I toss the sheets on the floor.

"Where are your clean sheets?" I ask.

"Hall closet." She sets the empty glass on the nightstand and puts her hand on my arm. Electricity ricochets from that spot all over my body, and she pulls back as if she felt it too. "I can get them."

"No, let me." I find the closet and grab a clean set and return to the room to make up her bed. I don't know why, but I want to take care of her, protect her.

"Why are you doing this?" she asks as I tuck in the flat sheet at the foot of the bed.

I don't answer but rather focus all my energy on finishing my task. When I'm done, I face her. Her tears have dried, and there's a little color back in her cheeks.

"Jett?"

"Hmm?"

"Are you going to answer me?"

How could I? My feelings for her make zero sense to me and would make even less to her.

"I should go." I turn away and walk to the door, sure that it's the right thing to do. The best thing to do.

The *only* thing to do.

7

EMMA

I stand there, motionless, watching him walk away, and with every step he takes, my heart thunders harder against my ribs, until there's nothing I can do but call him back.

"Wait!"

He stops but doesn't turn around. I go to him and block his exit.

"Please answer me." There's a begging quality to my voice and I hate it, even though I can't help it.

"I don't know how." He runs his hand through his hair, making it stand on end.

"Try. Please."

"Why? Why does it matter?"

"Because everything in me is telling me to make you go, that I don't want you here." I swallow past the lump in my throat. "But I haven't, and I don't understand why." I shrug, helpless to make the words mimic my thoughts. "Despite my fear, I'm still not letting you walk away."

"I'm not going to hurt you."

"Okay."

"You don't believe me."

"I don't know you."

"No, you really don't." He sighs and reaches out, but I back up a step. He drops his arms to his side, and it slaps against his thigh. "I heard you scream and came to make sure you were okay."

"You already told me that. Tell me something new."

"You were scared, crying and I just… I don't know." This man, who stands no less than a foot taller than me and is every bit of two hundred pounds of corded muscle, looks gutted.

"You do know." I have no idea why I'm pushing him, especially when a large part of me is afraid of him, of the power he exudes.

"The night of the riot, I didn't want to get involved. I tried. So fucking hard." His eyes search mine, and I give a slight nod to encourage him to continue. "But I couldn't let Lee hurt you like that. And then tonight, you screamed and every ounce of protectiveness I possess took over. Even now I can't shake it." He took a deep breath. "Thoughts of you got me through some pretty dark days in the last year and a half, and I just wanted to return the favor. Get you through the darkness."

I let his words sink in, infuse my soul with warmth. I want him to stay, at least until the darkness fades completely, but it never will and I know I have to let him go.

"Thank you. For making sure I was okay. But…" I let the unspoken words hang in the air between us.

"I know. I'm going." He steps around me, and I turn to watch him walk away… again. When he steps through the door, he looks over his shoulder and says, "You don't have to thank me. You never have to thank me for being there for you."

With those parting words, he continues his path to the

stairs, and when I don't hear the front door open and close, I walk to the steps and look down. He's standing there, staring at the splintered wood. He senses me staring and looks up at me.

"I'll get a piece of plywood to cover this and come back with a new door in the morning."

He disappears into the night, and I retreat to my bedroom and freshly made bed. I crawl under the covers and listen to the sounds of Jett pounding nails into his makeshift door. It's somehow comforting knowing he's still so close.

Silence finally ensues, and the last hour comes crashing back in. I try to hold back the tears and fail. I cry into my pillow, struggling to catch my breath. I cry for the woman who was assaulted in the prison. I cry for the woman who hides out from the world. I cry for the woman I'll never be.

I cry for me.

∽

It took me a while to get to sleep after Jett left. It was long after the sound of the hammer stopped that I was able to convince myself that I'd be safe behind the rickety barrier between me and the outside world.

Two hours of sleep is not at all enough for me to function like a person should, and it certainly isn't enough to handle the infernal pounding that's echoing off the walls. I shove up to my elbows and glare at my bedroom door. I know that Jett said he was going to be by this morning to put in a new door, but seriously? A glance at the clock tells me that it's only seven… way too damn early.

I throw my legs over the edge of the bed and stomp to the landing at the top of the stairs, hell-bent on demanding that he leave. As soon as he's in sight, all my bravado slithers away and I freeze. He's standing there with the new door held out in front of him like it's no heavier than a feather. His muscles are bulging, and he's not wearing a shirt.

A groan escapes past my lips, and he glances over his shoulder. He's wearing a look of concentration, but it's quickly replaced by a grin, complete with dimples.

"Mornin.'"

All of my good intentions fly out the window, and I stand there, staring, incapable of speech. I don't know if my cottonmouth was brought on by his insanely good looks or fear. Both, maybe?

"I'll be outta your hair in a few minutes." He looks at me with curiosity in his gaze and lifts the door a bit. "Just gotta hang this." When I remain silent, he starts to turn away from me but stops himself. The curiosity that was there a second ago morphs into concern. "Did you get much sleep last night after I... after?"

I shake my head and wrap my arms around myself. At the mention of what he witnessed, the temperature drops ten degrees.

"Right." He gives a sharp nod before turning to lean the door against the wall.

Once he's relieved of his burden, he doesn't return his attention to me. Not for a few minutes at least. I watch as he appears to have an internal debate with himself. He rubs the back of his neck before both his hands end up on his hips. His head falls forward, and I can practically hear the gears turning in his skull. When his hands drop to his sides, he whirls around to face me, and the pity in his eyes levels me.

"Look, I know that me being here makes you uncomfortable, and I'm sorry about that. There are things you don't know ab—"

"Don't." I hold up a hand but make no other movements. "I don't want your apologies or your explanations, and I sure as hell don't want your pity."

He flinches at my words. "Pity? I don't—"

"Don't lie to me." His eyes narrow in frustration, and I grip the banister in front of me, my knuckles turning white. "I can see it all over your face. And trust me, I know what it looks like."

"Maybe so, but—"

"And really, I don't blame you. You've seen me at my worst." My hands are cramping from the pressure in my grip, but I don't let up, needing to feel the pain, the reminder that I'm still alive. "But I'm fine now."

His brows raise as far up to his hairline as I imagine they'll go. "You're fine?"

"Yep. Never better." I try to hold his gaze, but I can't. I shift my focus to the wall behind him.

"Then why can't you look at me?"

I hear the creak of the stairs before it registers that he's walking toward me. I snap my gaze to his, and butterflies swarm in my stomach at the sight of him advancing.

"What are you doing?" I ask, a little too sharply.

"You said you're fine." He shrugs. "I'm testing that theory."

With each step he takes, I take one back, away from him and his infuriating… everything.

"You keep backing up, and I'm liable to think you're not fine." He pauses on the second to last step and tilts his head. "I suppose it could just be my imagination, but I doubt it."

"Why are you doing this?" The question is barely audible. The air is thick, making it almost impossible to breathe.

"Doing what?"

Tears burn and before I can stop it, one clings to my lower lashes before falling down my cheek. I furiously swipe at it, angry with him for doing this to me and pissed as hell at myself for letting him.

He stops walking. He thrusts a hand through his hair and sighs. When he returns his attention to me, the pity is gone, as well as the challenge. All that remains are emotions I know all too well: regret, pain, sadness. Which, as it turns out, are much harder for me to handle than pity.

"Emma, I'm sorry. I didn't mean—"

"Just… finish up and get outta here. Please." I spin and head for my bedroom, but before I can open the door, I look over my shoulder. He hasn't moved, but he's staring at the floor. "And, Jett?"

His head whips up at the sound of his name.

"Thanks for fixing the door."

With those parting words, I cross the threshold into my room, into safety, and slam the door. I flip the lock and lean back against the wood, letting my head fall back. I ignore the thud it makes as it connects. I slide down to the floor and draw my knees up to my chest, wrapping my arms around them.

Tears threaten, again, but I manage to hold them back. Several long minutes later, a knock startles me and I scramble up and face the barrier. I stare it down as if it was a rattlesnake that will strike at any second.

"Emma?" Jett's voice drifts through, and my shoulders sag.

Who did you think it was?

"Emma, c'mon, open the door." He doesn't knock again, and other than his voice and my pounding heart, there isn't another sound. Until he sighs and a small thump echoes through the door. I imagine it's his head, but I'm not about to open it and find out. "Em, I'm sorry. I don't know why I was pushing."

My hand flies to my mouth to stifle a cry. I don't know why his apology makes me want to cry, but I do know I don't want him to hear it.

"I'm gonna finish the door and I'll leave. I brought a pretty good lock, so I'll leave the keys on the kitchen counter." His footsteps tell me he's retreating, and when he continues, his voice sounds farther away. "I'll also write my phone number down, in case you need anything."

I nod before remembering that he can't see me.

"Use it or don't, makes no difference to me. But just know that you can. I'll be on the other end to answer if you need me."

I don't bother to hide the sob that erupts from me. My knees buckle, and I drop to the hardwood, ignoring the pain. I'm already damaged beyond repair.

What's a few more bruises?

8

JETT

Fucking smooth.

No matter how loud the drill was, how hard I swung the hammer, the sound of Emma's sobs couldn't be drowned out. I managed to get the door hung and the lock installed without going back upstairs to her bedroom, but it hadn't been easy.

"C'mon, Freedom." I give her the sign meaning 'come', and she trots to sit at my feet so I can snap the leash into place.

I left the keys on Emma's counter, just like I said I would. I debated on whether or not to leave my number and decided I'd better. I told her I would, after all.

Yeah, that's all there is to it.

Freedom dances around my feet, excitedly waiting for me to lead her out the back door. After finishing up at Emma's, I need to run off some of my excess energy and what better way to do that than with my dog? I could use the equipment in the basement, but Freedom needs the exercise too.

I let the latch on the back gate click into place and take off down the driveway and past Emma's house. I don't let my eyes wander to her newly installed door, but that doesn't stop my mind from wandering to the woman behind it.

I understand her reluctance to let a felon near her. Never mind that I'm not an actual criminal. *And saved her life.* What I don't get, what I can't quite wrap my mind around, is that she seems to have shut herself off from the world. Why? If it was only a few months after the riot, I'd get it, but it's been almost two years.

Freedom barks at another runner on the opposite side of the street, and the man waves. I wave back and give a little tug on the leash to urge Freedom to stay by my side. She hasn't had much socialization, at least not with me, and I need to work on that, but this morning is not the time.

I run ten miles, and when I return to the house, sweat is pooling at the base of my spine and my muscles are fatigued. The burn is welcome, and I know that I'm going to keep pushing myself, if for no other reason than it's been so long since I really enjoyed the ache of hard work.

Keep telling yourself that.

Fine. So I haven't managed to run Emma out of my head. She's still there, taking up what little space isn't dedicated to forgetting my own demons and learning how to be a part of a society that I've struggled to recognize since that last operation and quitting the DEA.

After feeding Freedom, I head downstairs to a space that is too reminiscent of the walls I lived behind for two years. The concrete floor, along with the cinder block walls, should make me feel trapped, but they don't. Instead, all I feel when I'm down here is a ridiculous sense of familiarity that calms me.

I take out my frustrations on the punching bag suspended from the ceiling before moving on to the weight bench. I don't lift as much as I can but enough to wear me out to the point of crashing. Before going back upstairs, I wipe everything down. I'm almost obsessive about the cleanliness of my space and won't be able to do anything else until that's done. When you're so used to such a confined area, being clean is required.

I let Freedom out into the backyard to do her business while I shower. Bracing my hands on the tile wall, I hang my head and let the hot water pelt my back. The warmth seeps into my muscles, and I feel the tension leaving my body. My thoughts circle back to Emma, and I stand there, unmoving, until it registers that the water has turned icy cold.

I slam my fists, knuckles out, into the wall and throw my head back to yell. The sound echoes around me, and when I drop my hands to my sides, I suck air through my clenched teeth at the sting as the water sluices over the now split flesh. Blood drips and swirls down the drain.

An image of the last time I was standing over a drain with blood being sucked down threatens to take hold, but I force it away. I step around the half-wall that makes up the 'door' to my shower and reach for a towel. I ignore the red spots appearing on the terrycloth and wrap it around my waist while I rinse my wounds and bandage them up with some gauze. I couldn't care less about how they heal, but I don't want to be tracking blood through the entire house.

As I'm walking down my steps to let Freedom back inside, I hear a car engine and look out the window. Emma's backing out of her driveway, but she's looking toward my house. Her eyes roam until they meet mine through the glass, and then she quickly looks away. I smile to myself as I continue my descent.

Maybe I scare her for reasons beyond simple fear. Maybe she's attrac—

I shake my head to ward off the thought. No way in hell is there more than fear. And not the good kind. When I get to the base of the steps, something catches my eye in the entryway. I glance down and see a piece of paper that appears to have been slid under the door and bend to pick it up.

The flowery writing throws me off but not for long.

Thank you for fixing my door. And for making sure I was okay last night. -E

So, she's been brave enough to leave this note, but only once she's sure she won't run into me. How did she know I was in the shower? Lucky guess, I suppose. I carry the note through the house and drop it on the kitchen counter on my way to the back door.

Freedom is barking, begging to be let in. I open the door and signal for her to sit. When she does, I give her a treat and, after making sure her food and water bowls are full, swipe the note off the counter and head to my bedroom.

I settle on top of the royal blue down comforter—one of several luxuries I succumbed to since purchasing the house—and hold the paper out in front of me. I read the words again, and then again, as if trying to decipher a hidden code between the letters. There isn't one. Big surprise.

I let my hands fall to my sides and blow out a breath. I don't know what it is about her, but Emma's gotten under my skin, weaved herself into every fiber of my being.

And she doesn't even know it.

~

I stare at the felon pacing the length of my cell.

"What the fuck were you thinking, Storm?"

"I dunno." I shrug. "I just couldn't sit back and watch Lee..." I can't even bring myself to say the words.

"That bitch was getting what she deserved."

I whirl around and wrap my hands around Tiny's throat. It isn't easy because Tiny isn't, well, tiny, but neither am I. The difference between the two of us is that he's mean as a snake and deserves to be behind bars while I'm just a cog in the wheel of justice.

"No one fucking deserves what he was going to do," I snarl.

Tiny's eyes are huge, and I can feel the vein in his neck throb, but I don't dare loosen my grip. Not yet.

"I'm only gonna say this once." *I glare at him and increase the pressure.* "If I ever hear you say that again... hell, if I ever hear you even so much as whisper her name, I'll gut you, consequences be damned. Ya feel me?"

I let up just enough so he can answer. At some point in the last two years, I've developed a felon mentality. I can chalk it up to maintaining my cover, but I'd be lying if I didn't admit that a part of me enjoys this persona.

"I feel ya," *he mumbles.*

"I can't hear ya, Tiny." *I arch a brow at him, taunt him.*

"I feel ya, Storm," *he says a bit louder.*

"Good."

I slam his head into the cinder block, only once, before I let him go. He scrambles to his bunk like the scared pussy I wish he was. I'm not stupid though. I know I just sealed my fate.

I toss and turn, moaning in my sleep, and my legs get tangled in the blanket. I try to reach out to the light in my mind, but the images shift and I'm sucked back into the nightmare.

The tepid water hits my back as I lather the soap into my hair. I'm facing the entrance to the showers for two reasons: it would be incredibly stupid of me not to and I heard rumblings in the cafeteria about retribution for my 'crazy, fucking stunt'.

I close my eyes and tip my head back to rinse my hair.

"Oh, whatta we got here, ladies?"

I tense at the unwelcome intrusion. I take in the crew before me, ignoring the burn of soap in my eyes. Santiago steps toward me, several of his crew following. Tiny's there and he darts his eyes back and forth between Santiago and me.

"Back from the hole I see," I taunt before pressing my lips together.

Instigating Santiago is stupid, but I can't help it. He and Lee were tight before the riot, and he always resented my 'relationship' with Lee. Now that his main squeeze is gone, it's not surprising that he's set his sights on me.

"Just in time to enter another," he sneers, his eyes dropping to my junk.

He licks his lips and fists himself. My skin crawls at the action, but I refuse to let him see my revulsion. I learned from watching him that he likes it when there's a little fight in his target.

"Aw, you miss your bitch, don't you?"

Santiago and his goons advance on me, two of them grabbing my arms and shoving me into the wall. I grind my teeth to keep from reacting to the pain.

"I'm gonna do to you what I know Lee wanted to do to the pretty little guard's cunt." Santiago's breath invades my nostrils, and I wrinkle my face. "And you're gonna like it."

My feet slip and slide as I'm twisted around so my chest is pressed against the faded green tile. The water has gone from tepid to freezing, and I pray for it to numb me. I no longer have any idea who's holding me in place, but whoever it is, their grip isn't as tight and I manage to put a few inches between me and the wall.

I hang my head, watching the water trickle to the drain, and will away my surroundings.

I lunge up from the bed, gasping for breath. The air is so thick that it's like trying to suck sludge through a straw. Once I'm able to breathe without the fear of passing out, I kick the covers away and stand on shaky legs.

I go to the window and throw it open, needing to smell something other than the rank stench of my sweat. The sun has started to set, and it casts an eerie glow over my view. I stare out at the yard for a long minute before I let my eyes wander to what they're really seeking.

Emma's car is back, and the lights are on in what I imagine is every room in the house. I want to go to her, beg for comfort and relief from *my* darkness. I crave it so much that I let my feet carry me to the front door. Before I can open it, Freedom's muted bark penetrates the fog and I stop.

What the fuck are you doing?

I shove my hands through my hair, and they come away damp. It's not like I haven't had that nightmare before, lived that day over and over in my head, but this time is different.

This time, my source of solace is so close and doesn't have to be just a memory.

9

EMMA

"You can't be serious."

I roll my eyes at Sierra for what seems like the hundredth time since the conversation began. It's movie night and two weeks since Jett fixed my door. When I remain silent, she keeps going like she's not about to drive me batshit crazier than I already am.

"So, not only does the guy save your life a few years ago, but he barges in here to rescue you from a monster he can't see and then fixes your door?" She takes a sip of her wine and holds up a finger to silence me when I open my mouth to speak. "He also plants you flowers, fixes your garage door—without being asked, I might add—and you *still* haven't talked to him for more than a few minutes?"

"I don't know what to say."

"How 'bout 'thank you'?" She shrugs. "Seems like a pretty good place to start."

"You don't get it." I stand up from the couch and start to pace, taking sips of my wine with each pass of the room.

"Oh, hon, I do get it." She stands up and starts to pace with me. Every step I take, she's right there by my side, letting me do what I need to while making sure I remember I'm not alone. "You're still so locked up in that moment, that one event that changed you, and you can't find your way out."

I glance at her but don't slow my steps.

"I'm starting to wonder if you *want* to stay there." She reaches out and taps my forehead. "At least there, you know the outcome. You don't have to wonder how it's all gonna end."

I stop pacing and grab her arm. "What are you talking about?"

Her lips curve into a sad smile, and her eyes soften. "You know I love you, right?" she says.

I nod, a lump suddenly forming in my throat because I know that she only says that when she's trying to warm me up to something I don't want to hear. She grabs my hands and squeezes them. Shit, this really is going to be bad.

"Do you remember when you got the job at the prison? How excited you were?"

I stare at her, wondering where this is going. When I don't respond, she continues.

"You were gonna go in there and be the kind of prison guard you said the world was missing. You were gonna care about them and be kind to them, but also be firm and in charge. Those were your words. You were so confident, so happy. Your family was terrified that you were making a mistake, but—"

"Turns out they were right."

"But," she draws out the word in her way of chastising me for the interruption. "You did it anyway. Because you were fearless." She chuckles. "Girl, when we were kids, you were the first one to do the scary thing and the last one to ever be scared. You were the first one to jump off the high dive, the first one to enter the haunted houses, the first to sleep in the cemetery on Halloween night, the first to kiss a boy... always the first." I let out a watery snort at the thought of our childish escapades. "Until you weren't."

"That's not fair," I protest.

"No, it's not." She shakes her head as she speaks. "But it's the truth. After the incident, you were hurt, terrified, and I told myself that you needed time to process everything. That you'd bounce back. But it's been almost two years, Em. *Two years.* You never went back to work—"

"I work!"

"You do medical billing from home. Yes, it's a job, and for a lot of people, it's the perfect job. But you're not a lot of people, and all it does is let you continue to hide out."

"It pays the bills, too." I know I'm latching on to anything that justifies why I do it, just like I know she's not going to stop telling me like it is.

"Sure. But so what? You have so much more to offer the world, so much to experience, yet you choose to let a few bad hours steal your life."

"You think I choose to be like this?" I yank my hands from hers and take a step back. Tears are silently streaming down my cheeks, and I swipe at them. "That I want to be this scared and lonely? Do you really believe that I don't want all of the things in life that I used to?"

"You tell me."

"Fine. I will." I turn away from her and walk to the window. I push the curtain aside and stare through the glass, sighing because I don't know how to describe how much I want to be out there. "I'm so tired, Si. I'm tired of being paralyzed by something that I can't change. I'm tired of watching the world move on without me. I'm tired of the sleepless nights and the nightmares that plague me when I *do* sleep. I'm tired of Sunday dinners with my family where everyone tiptoes around the elephant in the room." My breath hitches

JETT'S GUARD

when her hands rest on my shoulders. "I'm tired of it all. And I'm terrified that I'm destined to live this way forever. That I'll grow old and die alone."

Sierra grips my arms and urges me to turn around. When I'm facing her, her tears tell me that this conversation has taken a toll on her, as well. I hang my head, but she cups my cheeks and forces me to look at her.

"Then don't let that happen."

"I don't know what to do." I lift a shoulder, let it fall. "I don't know where to start."

"Aw, Em." The corners of her mouth lift into a sympathetic and encouraging smile. "Start by saying 'thank you.'"

∽

Two words.

That's it. Two words, out of the tens of thousands in the English language, and I want to throw up at the thought of saying them. It's not the words themselves. That's not the hard part. It's forcing myself to get close to the person I have to say them to.

I glance down at the slip of paper with Jett's phone number on it. My eyes dart between that and my phone.

C'mon, Emma. You can do this. Be fearless.

Sierra says I should go over to Jett's and thank him in person, but I'm not quite ready for that. Hell, I'm not even ready to call him and say the words out loud. But I can text. That isn't so scary and really, no different than what I do for work.

I blow out a breath and tap on the text icon. Seeing the very short list of people I text on a regular basis reminds me of why I have to do this. I wasn't lying when I told Sierra that I'm tired of being alone. I am, but that doesn't make doing something about it any easier.

I type in the digits of his phone number and enter a quick message: Thank you. I stare at the words for a few minutes, my thumb hovering over the send button, and debate if I should say more than that. Satisfied that it's enough, or at least a start, I let my thumb drop and the text registers as sent.

My heart rate picks up speed, and I take a few deep breaths to calm my nerves. I toss the phone onto the couch cushion next to me and get up to get a drink. If I don't, I'll stare at the screen and wait for a response. I pour a cup of coffee, and as I'm adding the creamer, my phone dings from the other room.

I force myself to finish my task. I want to race to the living room and see what he texted back but don't. Once I'm sure my coffee is doctored perfectly, I allow my curiosity to get the best of me and rush to the couch, careful not to slosh any of the hot liquid onto my hand. I snatch my cell up with my free hand and sit down before I let myself look at it.

I take a sip of my coffee and set the mug on the table, curling my legs under me after I do. I take a deep breath and turn the phone so I can see the screen and then tap it to bring it to life. My brow furrows when I read the words.

Who is this?

Well, shit. I didn't take into consideration that he doesn't know my number. I drop my head into my hands and shake it, disgust filtering through at my lack of forethought. A five-minute pep-talk later, I text him back.

Emma

Three dots appear, and I stare at them, holding my breath. They disappear. Maybe he knows more than one Emma? I send a text to clarify.

Emma Jordan.

Shit! I hit send before it occurred to me that he probably

doesn't know my last name. Three dots appear and then disappear... again. I type a quick clarification... again.

Your neighbor

I lean my head back and let out a groan. If Jett doesn't already think I'm a weirdo, he will now. I silently berate myself, and after the sixth *you're such an idiot*, my phone dings. My head snaps up, and I lift the cell to read the text.

Ah, okay. What are you thanking me for?

Seriously?!

Of course he would be the type that needs it spelled out for him. My anxiety lessens and is replaced with frustration. I start to type my response and notice that he's typing something too. Before I can finish, his text appears.

Kidding...

What the actual fuck? Does he not realize how difficult this is for me? Frustration morphs into blinding anger, and before my actions register, I'm marching across the yard and stomping up his front steps.

I pound a fist on the door and stand there, tapping my foot while I wait for him to answer. It takes him a few minutes, but when the door swings open, my foot stills and my jaw drops.

What the hell are you doing?

My inner voice is screaming at me, but I don't have the answer. One minute, I'm scrambling to make sure he knows who's texting him and the next I'm staring at him, in the flesh. And what flesh it is.

"Take a picture. It'll last longer."

I slam my mouth shut and force my eyes to meet his. He's wearing a shit-eating grin and doesn't look the least bit uncomfortable. But why should he? He's freaking magnificent. Every inch of him is perfect, even the scar on his lower abdomen.

"Emma?" His grin disappears, and his forehead wrinkles in concern.

All of a sudden, I remember why I'm here. I thrust my phone out, screen facing him.

"Kidding? You were kidding?!" I screech. "Do you have any clue how hard it was for me to text you?"

He reaches out to lower my arm. "Why don't you come inside?"

He steps to the side and sweeps his arm out to encourage me in. My eyes dart back and forth between his face and the empty space that would allow me to enter. He drops his arm and sighs.

"You made it this far. What's a few more feet?"

I swallow past the lump in my throat. I'm equal parts terrified and curious when it comes to this man. I was perfectly happy with my life before he moved in. A hermit, maybe, but I hadn't questioned it. My life was what it was. But now?

"If you don't want to come in, do you mind if I at least go put on some clothes? It's a little cold out here."

As much as I want to, I can't quite bring myself to cross the threshold. Instead, I turn around and scurry down the steps and back to my house, back to safety and the familiar. I slam my door behind me and engage the lock.

I take a step back and stare at the wooden barrier. The beautiful mahogany mission-style door that Jett installed. The one that fits my house perfectly and had to have cost a small fortune. Granted, he destroyed my previous door, but his replacement is so much better.

The back of my eyes burn. I think about everything he's done for me, going back to the night of the riot, and hang my head. Maybe I am a lost cause. Maybe I should just throw in the towel and tell Sierra that I can't do it.

Maybe, maybe, maybe.

A thumping sound startles me, and my head snaps up. I hear it again and realize someone's knocking, demanding to be heard. My limbs begin to shake, and my vision blurs.

"Emma, c'mon, open up." Jett's voice registers and everything comes back into focus. "I'm sorry I made a joke. I didn't mean to upset you."

I rush to the door and open it a crack. He's put on clothes —a forest green Henley that brings out his eyes and dark wash jeans—and looks very upset. He rubs the back of his neck and quirks up one side of his mouth.

"Can I come in?" When I make no move to let him enter, he says, "Just for a minute… please?"

I don't know if it's against my better judgement or not, but I step aside to let him in. He crosses the threshold and takes in his surroundings. I follow his gaze, wondering what my space says about me. What he might learn from it.

"Nice place." He's standing next to the couch, and suddenly everything I own seems so small. "It suits you."

"You don't know me," I say and then slam my mouth shut.

"Touché," he chuckles. It's a nice sound, warm, genuine.

I take a deep breath and close the distance between us. My hands are clasped in front of me, and I can't quite bring myself to look him in the eye.

"I'm sorry ab—"

"You don't have to apologize." He reaches out, and I quickly step away, avoiding the contact. He sighs and drops his arm. "I'm sorry I made a joke. I didn't know it would upset you so much."

I remain silent, not sure what to say.

"Why did it upset you?" he asks.

That's not an easy question to answer, so I stall. "Can I get you something to drink?"

His brows dip down in confusion. "Uh, sure. Coffee if you have it. I haven't had any yet."

I rush around him to the kitchen and make a fresh pot. Once it's percolating, I grip the counter and make no move to return to the living room.

"Emma?" I jump at the sound of his voice, so close behind me. "I, uh, know you're scared, but I'm not going to hurt you."

"I know." And surprisingly, I do. But that doesn't mean that I can just will away the fear that I've held onto for so long.

"Do you? Because your actions say otherwise."

I turn around to face him, but no words pass my lips. He takes a step toward me. My instinct is to back up, but the counter prevents me from doing that.

"Look, can we maybe start over?"

"How?" My brow wrinkles in confusion.

"Hi. I'm Jett Stover." He thrusts his hand out for me to shake. "And you are?"

A small smile plays on my lips, and I cautiously slip my hand into his, my skin tingling at the contact. I suck in a breath before saying, "I'm Emma. Emma Jordan."

The introduction feels silly, but it has the effect I imagine he intended and my nerves settle.

"Nice to meet you, Emma Jordan." He reluctantly releases my hand and shoves both of his in his pockets. He rocks back on his heels and laughs when I don't say anything. "You're supposed to follow that up with 'nice to meet you too, Jett'."

I shake my head. "Right. Um, it's nice to meet you too, Jett."

The coffee pot beeps, indicating that the brew is ready. I busy myself making us both a cup, and while I doctor mine, he leaves his black.

"This is good," he mumbles around the rim of his mug. "What kind is it?"

"Starbucks Breakfast Blend." I shrug. "Nothing special."

"Right." He takes another hearty sip. "Never had anything this good in the cage."

I choke on the liquid sliding down my throat. My eyes water and I cough until I'm able to catch my breath.

"Sorry." His smile from earlier is gone, in its place a look of regret. "Here we are trying to start over, and I go and stick my damn foot in my mouth."

I wave my hand in front of my face. "No, no. It's fine."

"It's not, but thanks for saying so."

I give a sharp nod and push off the counter to walk to the living room. The kitchen is smaller and with us both in it, it's miniscule. He follows me, and we sit on opposite ends of the couch. We remain silent for several minutes before I can't take it any longer.

"So, what now?"

He chuckles and the sound curls around me, seeps into my bones.

"I have some thoughts on that," he says. His gaze is focused on my face, and I force myself to return it.

"Okay." I draw the word out.

"Since we're starting over and everything, maybe we could get to know each other."

"Like a date?"

"No, not a date." He glances away like he's not sure if that was the right thing to say. "Like friends. No pressure. No strings."

Sierra's voice invades my head, telling me to go for it, that I can't have too many friends. That I should take a chance. But it's not that easy.

"Jett, it's not that easy for me." I dart my tongue out to lick my lips. "I, um…" I glance toward the door, wishing it were as simple as walking through it.

"You're doing great right now." His words have me swinging my head back to him, and his lips tip up at the corners. He tilts his head and says, "It doesn't take a genius to figure out you don't like to go out. And I get it. But what if we just spent time here? In your own space?"

I let his words swirl around in my brain before making a decision that I'm not sure I won't regret. Sierra would be so proud.

"Okay. Yeah." I lick my lips again. "I can do that."

His grin widens. "Good." He pushes to his feet and takes his empty mug to the sink. When he returns, he stops before he can pass the couch. "You cook?"

"I, uh, yes."

"I can grill a damn good steak, but the rest? Not so much." He walks to the door and opens it. Before he leaves, he looks over his shoulder. "You do have a grill, right?"

I nod.

"Great. I'll bring the meat, and you handle the rest. Six o'clock work for you?"

I quickly search my mind for any plans I might have. *Who are you kidding? You're more than wide open, and you know it.*

"Sounds good."

"See ya later, then." He walks out the door, pulling it closed behind him.

I sit there for what feels like forever, dumbfounded.

What the hell just happened?

10

JETT

I glance at my phone to check the time.

Great. It's 4:07pm, which is only four minutes later than the last time I checked. I shake my head, mentally chastising myself for not relaxing.

I don't know what possessed me to invite myself over to Emma's for dinner, but there's no backing out now. Who am I kidding? I know exactly what I was thinking. Emma is a beautiful woman, and we have a history. Sort of. And there's something about her that I can't quite shake.

I push off the couch and go to get ready for our date. Wait, not a date. Just a dinner between two people who can't even really be described as friends. Freedom follows me to the bathroom and lays down on the dog bed I put in there for her. She likes to be close to me so she might as well be comfortable. Besides, having her nearby makes me feel less alone.

I sift through my dresser, trying to find something to wear for this non-date date. It's not my intention to put her on edge or for tonight to be anything but relaxing, so I settle on a white T-shirt and jeans. I look at myself in the mirror and groan when my reflection mocks me.

You can do better than that.

I turn back to find something else and realize that no, I can't do much better. I yank a red plaid flannel from the drawer and shove my arms through the sleeves. I study myself in the mirror one more time. Good enough.

Back downstairs, I check the time again and am horrified to see that I've only managed to kill half an hour. It's still way too early for me to show up on her doorstep. I decide to take Freedom for a walk and pray that it will also serve to calm my nerves.

An hour later, I'm back inside and not much calmer. *Jesus, how do people do this?* It's been so long since I've been with a woman, not to mention been *just friends* with one. Before going undercover in the prison, I had numerous other undercover assignments. I had women, sure, but they weren't the type I wanted to be linked to for more than the time it took to satisfy us both. And there hasn't been any woman since before the prison.

I shake off my past and focus on getting the steaks out of the fridge. I marinated them all day, and the smell that wafts from the container has my stomach growling. I let Freedom outside one last time before heading next door.

While I wait for Emma to answer the door, my stomach twists into knots. I can't shake the feeling that, despite trying to convince myself otherwise, this dinner is monumental. For me and for her.

When the door swings open, my gaze snaps to hers and my mouth goes dry. Chocolate brown eyes stare back at me and in them I see a nervousness that matches my own. I let my eyes drift down her body and take in her form-fitting black sweater and tight jeans. Her feet are bare, and she's painted her toenails a bright red. For some reason, that makes me smile, and when I return my scrutiny to her face, a blush creeps into her cheeks.

"Wow." I manage to push that one word past my lips.

"Maybe this wasn't a good idea," she blurts out.

Her lips are drawn into a tight line and she's wringing her hands to the point that her knuckles are turning white from the pressure. She's scared as hell. All of my earlier nerves disappear as my senses are invaded by an intense desire to protect. I remember that she warmed up quicker this morning when I railroaded her, so that's what I do now.

"Nah. It was a great idea."

I squeeze past her and let myself into her living room, not giving her a chance to stop me. I head straight for the kitchen and deposit the steaks on the counter. The smell of, I don't even know what, hangs in the air, and I breathe it in, enjoying the deliciousness it promises.

When I return to the living room, Emma's standing behind the couch, gripping the back. The blush is gone and she's pale. She's looking everywhere but at me, and I know I need to get this situation under control. Fast.

"Emma, look at me," I say as I walk toward her.

Her eyes dart around, but before she can meet my gaze, she drops her head.

"Please." When I reach her, I reach out and lift her chin so she's forced to face me. When I'm sure I have her full attention, I move my hand to her shoulder and let it rest there. "You have complete control over the evening, okay? Nothing is going to happen. We're gonna eat, talk, maybe even laugh a little." One corner of my mouth tips up. "And when you want me to leave, I will. But for now, try to relax."

In the back of my mind, I know one piece of information would calm her down. If she knew that I was undercover in the prison and not the scary bad guy that she thinks, I'm fairly certain that would help. But I've tried to tell her and for whatever reason, the words never leave my mouth. Not only that, but a part of me doesn't want to tell her because then I'd have to talk about other things I'm not quite ready to talk about.

Her lids slide closed, and she takes a deep breath, swallows it down. I watch the lines of her throat, see the pulse point throbbing. My dick hardens behind my zipper, and I quickly shift to adjust myself, grateful that she can't see it.

"Sierra says I need to do this." Her eyes are still closed, but some color is returning to her cheeks.

"Sierra sounds like a smart woman." I let my arm fall to my side, and her eyes snap open the second I break contact.

"She's a pain in my ass." Finally, a smile graces her face. "But yeah, pretty smart."

"You love her."

"Of course I do." The simple statement is followed by a wide grin, and my knees threaten to buckle at the beauty of it. Of her. "She's my best friend. More than that, really. She's the one person that hasn't let…" She slams her mouth shut, and her eyes grow wide.

The emotion that passes through her eyes tells me that there's so much that she'd been about to say, so much I want to explore, but I let it go. We'll get there eventually, and my instincts tell me to let her set the pace of our conversations.

"I gotta tell ya, whatever you got going in the kitchen smells incredible." I step away from her, giving her space. "If you point me in the direction of the grill, I'll get the steaks on. Don't know about you, but I'm fucking starved." I already know the grill is on her back deck, but I ask anyway.

Emma stares at me a moment longer before shaking her head. Her feet seem to come unglued from their spot, and she brushes past me to the kitchen, looking over her shoulder to see if I follow. It's a no brainer. I follow.

"Grill's out back." She points at the French doors that lead to her deck. "I don't use it much, so I hope it works."

She busies herself with taking the steaks out and putting them on a platter for me. I open the door and step outside to make sure everything works. I can cook the steaks in a cast iron skillet, in a pinch, but I'm better with a grill.

Light footsteps catch my attention, and I throw a glance over my shoulder to see Emma carrying the platter. The breeze catches her blonde hair, lifts it from her neck, exposing the column of her throat. Her creamy complexion ignites a fire in me, and I silently beg for the boner-gods to stay away.

"Grill seems to be working." I relieve her of her burden. "Shouldn't take too long to cook." She shoves her now empty hands in her back pockets, and I itch to join my hands with hers. "How do you like your steak?"

"Oh, um, medium."

"You got it."

I get to work on the meat, and she returns inside. I still have no idea what she's prepared, but if the smell is any indication, it's gonna be good. As I stand there, I look through the glass of the doors a few times, wanting to catch a glimpse of Emma as she sets the table. Clattering dishes and silverware punctuate her movements.

When the steaks are done, I shut off the grill and take them inside. The French doors lead into the space Emma's set up to serve as a dining room, and my jaw drops. She's prepared a small feast. My mouth waters as I look from one dish to the next. Fluffy mashed potatoes, two baked potatoes, corn, salad, baked macaroni and cheese, green beans, and dinner rolls are all arranged across the table, with two place settings, complete with linen napkins.

"Holy shit," I mumble.

"I wasn't sure what you liked." My head whips up at the sound of her voice. Her cheeks darken to a rosy hue.

"This. I like this." I set the platter of steaks down in the only empty space, smack dab in the center of everything else.

"Are you sure? Because I can make something else if—"

"Emma, it's great." I step toward her, cautiously. "It's perfect."

"I know you said this wasn't a date." She pauses, takes a deep breath, drops her head. "But it's been a while since I've cooked for anyone other than Sierra, and I figured it had been a while since you had a home-cooked meal, and I was worried that—"

"Emma." My tone is sharp, and she lifts her gaze to peer at me. "First, not a date." *Oh, but you want it to be.* "Second, everything looks great. Third, relax. It's just me."

She groans before crossing her arms over her chest. "That's the problem. I don't know you."

"Then let's change that." I urge her toward a chair and pull it out for her. "Is there anything else that we need?" I ask once she's seated.

She shakes her head. "No."

"Okay."

I sit in the chair across from her. I fork a steak onto each of our plates and sit back to wait for her to serve herself first. I may not have been on a lot of dates in a while, but I'm not a moron. When she makes no move to get more food, I start doing it for her. When both of our plates are full, I dig in. I may not be a moron, but I am hungry. Maybe if I eat, she will too.

After a few minutes, she begins to take small, tentative bites. We go on like this for a bit before I break the silence.

"So, tell me about yourself."

Her fork pauses halfway to her mouth, the last bite of steak hovering on the tines, and tilts her head.

"What do you want to know?"

Everything.

I shrug. "Whatever you want to tell me, I guess."

She chews her food and takes a sip of water after she swallows it down.

"Well, there's not much to tell." She smoothes her fingers over the edge of the table. "I'm twenty-nine. I like dogs but am allergic to cats. I have a degree in criminal justice, but I work in customer service. My favorite color is—"

A snort escapes and she narrows her eyes at me.

"What?"

"Nothing. It's just… let me guess, you like long walks on the beach, holding hands at the movie theater and candlelit dinners."

"Well, I suppose but I haven't really—"

"You're not filling out a dating site profile." When she looks at me with confusion, I clarify. "Just… I have an idea. How 'bout we play twenty questions? That way you don't have to struggle to come up with what to say and you can also ask me anything you want."

She rests her chin in her hand, elbow on the table. She seems to be thinking about whether or not this is a trap. It's not. I genuinely want to get to know her. She'll figure that out soon enough.

"Okay," she agrees. "I get to go first, though."

"Fair enough." I toss my napkin onto the table and lean back in my chair. "Shoot."

"How tall are you?"

I throw my head back and laugh. "Seriously? That's your question?"

"I'm starting out with the easy ones." She shrugs.

"Fine. I'm six foot three." Her eyes widen a fraction. "And just so you don't have to waste any more of your questions, I'll throw in some freebie info. I'm just shy of two hundred and ten pounds, all muscle." I punctuate my statement with a wink, and she reaches for her water to guzzle some down. "My turn. Where did you grow up?"

"I grew up around here. Just on the other side of town."

"Any siblings?"

"A younger brother, Elijah." Sadness filters into her expression, but she quickly masks it. "That was two questions so now I get two… same ones you just asked me."

"Grew up in Indiana."

"Any siblings?" she asks when I don't give her the information.

"I had a brother." My stomach drops, as it always does when the conversation goes in this direction. "Harrison."

"Had?"

"He's dead." I don't offer any explanation, no further details, just a flat statement that I hope she accepts and moves on.

"I'm sorry. I didn't know."

"No problem." I inject as much levity into my tone as I can. It's not her fault that anything related to Harrison sets me on edge. "My turn."

"Don't do that."

"Do what?"

"Pretend that I didn't just bring up what is obviously a very painful thing for you." She chews on her bottom lip before releasing it. "If anyone can understand pain and not wanting to talk about it, it's me."

And her issues are something I promised myself I wouldn't bring up, so I ask my question.

"What's your family like?"

She sighs and there's a tinge of frustration in it. "For the most part, they're great. My mom's a high school math teacher, and my dad's a retired mechanic. Elijah is two years younger than me. He got married last year, and they bought a little house on the same street we grew up on. We're a pretty average family. We were all really close until, well..." She lets the words drift away and shrugs. "Now family dinners are awkward, but it's not their fault. They just have no idea how to act around me, what to say."

"That actually sounds nice. I mean, not the awkward part but everything else." My parents had been like that, at one point. Then everything changed. God, that feels like a lifetime ago.

"Yeah, I guess. I wish things were like they used to be, though." She glances past me, and I turn my head to see what she's looking at. A family picture. Her gaze returns to me. "Anyway, my turn." She tilts her head, appearing to think very hard about her next question. "How'd you get your nickname? Storm?"

Shock spreads through me. I didn't expect her to bring up anything related to the prison. "It's pretty stupid, actually. Turns out, inmates aren't that creative, and the ones I've come into contact with are pretty stupid. I don't even remember who it was, but someone made a joke about my name, thought Jett Storm was the funniest thing ever said, and it stuck. I think he was thinking of the phrase 'Jet stream', but I let it go because most newbies thought it was something more sinister and they didn't bother me."

She grins, the crease at the corners of her eyes become more pronounced, and the next thing I know, she's laughing. She waves her hand in front of her face and manages to suck in a few deep breaths to calm down.

"I'm sorry. It's just... it's so ridiculous." Her laughter renews, and I let her go. When she lets her guard down, she's beautiful, carefree, and I don't want to ruin it.

"Told ya."

While she works to get herself under control, I stand and start to clear away the dishes. By the time she does, the table is completely bare of any remnants of our dinner. I pull out her chair and urge her to stand so we can shift to the living room and continue our conversation.

When we're both seated at opposite ends of the couch, I dive back in.

"Favorite color?"

"Red. You?"

"Blue. Favorite food?"

"Mint chocolate chip ice cream. Favorite candy?"

"Gummy worms."

We go back and forth like that until I know her favorite flower, movie, book, restaurant, and smell. I commit the answer to memory, vowing to use them to my advantage. Neither of us ask anything serious, but the questions are there, lingering in the air waiting to be plucked down and given voice to. She's the first one to take the chance, which surprises the hell out of me.

"Why did you save me?"

My eyes snap to hers, and my chest constricts. That isn't a question I'm prepared to answer. It isn't that the answer is a difficult one, but this is the beginning of a conversation that will end the night.

"It was the right thing to do?" My answer comes out in the form of a question, despite it being the truth. Well, part of the truth.

"Yeah, maybe it was, but I don't think that's why." She pulls her knees to her chest and wraps her arms around them. "Len didn't do shit to help. And he fucking worked there!" She shakes her head in disgust. "And you weren't going to step in. Not at first."

"Len was a pussy. 'Scuse my language, but it's true." I pause, trying to come up with the words to explain it to her. "It *was* the right thing to do. No woman deserves what he was trying to do to you, but you're right, I was going to sit back and do nothing. Lee's a prick and definitely not someone I wanted to piss off, but…" I shrug. "I don't know. At first, you were fighting, ready to take on anything. And then you stopped. I hated seeing you give up."

"I wanted to die," she whispers. She swipes at a tear I hadn't seen fall. "He enjoyed the fight, and I didn't want to give it to him."

Her entire demeanor has changed in the last few minutes. She's withdrawing from me and closing herself up. I take a chance and scoot closer to her. She has nowhere to go to get away, unless she stands, but she doesn't. Her eyes are wide, frightened.

"Aw, doll. We've been through this. I'm not going to hurt you." I extend my arm and let my hand rest on her knee.

She glances at it, and I can feel her internal struggle. The debate about whether or not she should enjoy my touch or shy away from it. She raises her eyes to me, and there's a sheen over them, but she's resisting it, not letting the tears fall. I can't stand her fear, so I make a snap decision to put everything out there.

"Emma, there are things you don't know about me." I rub circles over her kneecap. "I'm not—"

"Jett, I…"

"Hmm? You what?"

"I…" She gives in and shoves up from the couch, away from me. "I can't do this." Her bare feet beat a hushed thump across the hardwood floor. "I thought I could, and it wasn't so bad, but now I can't."

I stand and go to her, but she holds up a hand to stop me.

"Don't. I, uh, I think you should go." One hand is gripping the hem of her sweater and the other is fidgeting with the silver chain around her neck. "Please."

As I stand there, dozens of arguments race through my mind, and I know I could convince her to let me stay, but I don't say any of them. Tonight was a huge step for her, that much is clear, and I've already decided to let her set the pace.

It's weird, this need to let her dictate how things go, this drive to protect her even when it costs me so much. But just because it's weird doesn't mean it isn't right.

"I'll leave." I walk toward the door and pause before opening it and glance back at her. "I had fun tonight, and I'm sorry everything fell apart."

"M-me too," she stutters.

"Call me if you need anything."

I leave her with those words and go back to my place. Freedom rushes to greet me, and I spend an hour with her in the backyard, throwing the ball around in the dark and waiting for her to bring it back to me. Once she's worn out, we both head upstairs.

I strip as I'm walking, and by the time I reach the bed, I'm naked. I tug the covers down and crawl in, lying on my back to stare at the ceiling. I replay the night with Emma, over and over in my mind, trying to determine if there was something I could have done differently. Something I should've done.

You should have told her the truth.

Knowing my conscience is right, I think about what to do next. Leave her alone? Keep trying to be her friend? Force her to listen to me when I try to tell her the truth? Go through Sierra? Everything and nothing sounds like a good idea, and by the time the sun rises, I've managed to get zero sleep.

It was worth it though because now, I have a plan.

11

EMMA

"There's my baby girl."

The arms around me tighten, and I roll my eyes. I'm twenty-nine and my family still talks to me like I'm five.

"Hey, dad."

I ease back and look at the man who raised me. He's not a big man, just shy of six feet, but he's always been a giant to me. Unless my mom is in the room, and then he's reduced to mush. But as I stare at his face, examine the wrinkles that always seem to increase in numbers, I'm reminded that he's aging and won't be around forever.

"I thought you'd forgotten about us." He looks over his shoulder and calls for my mom. "You haven't been here in a few weeks."

"I've been busy." We both know that's a lie, that I'm never busy since *it* happened. But bless him, he lets it slide. "And besides, I'm here now."

I paste a smile on my face and turn to hug my mom when she steps up next to him.

"Oh, honey, we've missed you," she whispers when her arms come around my neck.

I laugh at them and push back.

"It's been three weeks, not years. And I'm just on the other side of town. It's not like I'm on a different planet."

"Ya sure about that?"

I whirl around and smack Elijah on the arm. Even though we're adults, he still plays the part of pain-in-the-ass-younger-brother to perfection.

"C'mon, you guys. You know where I live. You could come visit me."

And just like that, tension fills the room because no one knows what to say. They know
why I stay home. They know what it means when I miss a few weeks' worth of family dinners. Everyone is quiet and my parents and brother are looking at each other like they're taking silent bets on who's going to bring it up first. I know none of them will so I change the subject.

"I'm starving." I breeze by them like nothing happened. And really, nothing did. "What're we having for dinner?" I call over my shoulder because the three of them are rooted to their spots.

Finally, Elijah's feet come unglued and he approaches the dining room, plastering a stupid grin on his face. My parents follow suit.

"Your dad's gonna grill some steaks, and I've got baked potatoes in the oven," Mom says as she moves past me into the kitchen.

At the mention of steaks, my shoulders sag. The last time I ate that was with Jett. I haven't spoken to him since, although he continues to do little things for me and has called and texted several times.

"Sis, you okay?" Elijah puts a hand on my forearm, and when I glance at him, there's a look of concern.

"Yeah. Fine." I shake away my thoughts. "Why wouldn't I be?"

Elijah takes my hand and tugs me toward the screened in back porch. We've spent so much time here over the years, talking, venting, reminiscing. Whenever there's a family dinner or holiday and we need an escape, we come out here to get away. We've always been close and can tell each other everything, but this is the first time in a few years he's brought me out here.

"Why'd you bring me out here?" I cross my arms over my chest and narrow my eyes at him.

Elijah's hands are in his pockets, and he looks out over the yard beyond the mesh barriers. The sound of our parents bickering drifts through the sliding screen door, and it's somehow comforting. If the words are any indication, Dad's trying to sneak a snack and Mom's having none of it. Nothing too out of the ordinary.

"Elijah?" I relax my stance and step up next to him.

"I hate that I feel like I have to tiptoe around you," he exclaims before turning his head to focus his attention on me. "I miss you, Em. The way you used to be. The way *we* used to be."

I'm taken aback by his words. I know things have been different since the riot, but I didn't realize it had this much of an impact on him.

"I'm sorry, but I can't do it anymore." He starts to pace and as I watch him, I realize how much like our dad he is. Sweet, gentle, loyal... stubborn. "Mom mentioned steak, and your face went white as a sheet, and my instinct was to tease you about it but I couldn't. I miss when I wouldn't have thought twice about it."

My lungs deflate at the frustration in his voice. It's one thing for my life to be turned upside down, but the lives of my family? That's not something I'm prepared to handle or something I even considered.

"Aren't you going to say anything?" Elijah demands when he comes to a stop in front of me.

"I don't know what to say," I tell him honestly. "I never asked for this, for any of it. I never wanted everyone to treat me like I'd break at any moment and I—"

"That's just it! You do break, at the littlest things, and I don't like being part of the breaking. Neither does mom and dad."

"You don't understand," I mutter.

"What's to understand?" He grips my shoulders and forces me to look at him. "There was a riot, and you were hurt. Pretty badly but not as badly as you could've been. You got out. Someone made sure you got out, alive and in one piece." He blows out a breath and drops his arms. "Don't get me wrong, I was terrified when I got the phone call. Tracy had to drive me to the hospital because I was a wreck, thinking the worst." At the mention of his wife, I realize she's not here and I make a mental note to ask him about that. "I stayed in the hospital with you until you were released. I had to convince Mom and Dad to leave so they wouldn't hover or worse, make themselves sick with worry. And then you came home, and I thought 'Good, she's gonna be fine. She'll bounce back because that's how Emma works. She's a fighter.'. And you got better physically, but mentally you stayed in a dark hole and you haven't come out since."

Tears are streaming down my face, and I swipe at the wetness. At that moment, I make a snap decision and open up to my brother for the first time in a long time.

"I had a date," I blurt out before I can think twice about it.

He stares at me, his eyebrows practically touching his hairline, and a grin slowly spreads across his face.

"Yeah?"

"Well, kinda. Maybe. Not really a date," I stammer. "I had dinner with a guy, and he said it wasn't a date, but it felt like a date."

"You're gonna have to back up and slow down." He pulls his cell phone out of his pocket and taps the screen.

"What're you doing?" I ask.

"Calling Tracy. She's going to want to hear this." There's excitement in his voice as he scrolls through his contacts.

"Not yet." I place my hand over his to stop him. He looks at me with confusion so I rush to explain. "It's hard enough for me to talk to one person about it, let alone two. Please, let me get this out to you first."

He nods and puts his phone down. "Okay."

"Where is she by the way? She's usually here."

"She wasn't feeling well, so she stayed home." At my look of concern, he adds, "Nothing to worry about, I promise." He's lying. Elijah has never been able to lie to me, but this time, I don't call him on it. He quirks a brow at me. "And you're stalling."

I huff out a breath. "Fine." Maybe I am stalling, but I do really want to know where my sister-in-law is. "He's my neighbor, Jett. He, uh, he's been doing things for me. Planting flowers, fixing stuff." I flap a hand at that because it's a minute detail of the story. "When I tried to thank him, it went epically wrong." I groan as the scene I made on his porch floods my mind.

"Must not have been too bad because you had dinner with him."

"I made a fool of myself, and it ended with him coming over and inviting himself to dinner."

"Why do I have the feeling that you're leaving a whole shitton of the details out?" A smile tugs at the corners of his mouth.

"Anyway," I say, drawing the word out. "He came over for dinner that night and—"

He snaps his fingers, cutting me off. "That's why you looked like you'd seen a ghost when I mentioned steak. That's what you had that night, with him."

I nod and continue my story. "He said it was just a way to get to know each other, be friends, and Sierra's been pushing me to do more so I agreed. Not that he gave me much of a choice. And it was going really well until…"

When I remain silent, he grabs my hand and squeezes it, encouraging me to continue.

"Until I brought up the riot," I whisper.

"Why did you bring it up?" he asks with genuine interest. I peer at him and silently plead with my eyes for him to not make me say it. "C'mon, Em. It's me. You can tell me anything, you know that."

I take a deep breath, and before I can think twice, I push the words out. "Jett is Storm."

Elijah's eyes narrow, as if he's trying to place the name, and then they grow wide. "Holy shit."

"Yeah."

"Wow. Okay, so the guy that saved you during the riot is your neighbor. I did *not* see that coming."

"Me either." I avert my gaze and stare out beyond him.

The smell of Dad grilling is in the air, and it'll be time to eat soon. I don't say a word, letting the information dangle between us while Elijah seems to be sorting through it. He finally breaks the silence.

"I mean, it's not a bad thing, if you think about it. He's the one person that understands what you've been through. He was *there*, Em. You don't have to hide from him."

"That's almost exactly what Sierra said."

"Well, she's not wrong." The shock seems to have worn

off, conviction in its place. "So, what happened after you brought up the riot?"

"Take one guess."

"You freaked," he says, sure of himself. Well, he's not wrong.

"I made him leave. And I haven't talked to him since."

"What?!" Elijah rears back as if he's been slapped. "Why?"

"Because," I shout, pulling away from him and beginning to pace. "I'm damaged and he knows it! He knows *exactly* how much. Why would he want anything to do with me?"

"Why *wouldn't* he? That's what you need to ask yourself. No man in their right mind could take one look at you and not see a good thing. You're not damaged. Just scarred a bit. And that's okay."

I hear what he's saying, soak up his words and try to process them.

"I want you to do something." He holds up a hand to stop me when I try to speak. "First, I'm going to tell you something that you have to promise not to tell mom and dad."

"Okay," I say in confusion.

"You have to promise."

"I promise." Worry surfaces at the seriousness in his eyes. "Is something wrong? Is Tracy okay?"

"Nothing's wrong and she's fine." He takes a deep breath, blows it out. "She's pregnant."

I let out a squeal and throw my arms around him. "That's great! I'm so happy for you guys." He returns my hug, and we stay like that for a moment, soaking up the good. Then a question forms. "Wait, why are you telling me? You obviously weren't planning to. Is that why Tracy's home sick? Is something wrong with the baby?"

He chuckles and then covers my mouth with his hand to shut me up. "I told you, Tracy's fine. The baby's fine." He drops his hand, and his smile turns sad. "I'm telling you because you needed to hear something positive. I'm telling you because you're going to be an aunt. And I'm telling you because our baby is going to need you, *all* of you." He pauses, lets that sink in. "Emma, Sierra's right. It's time to live a little. If not for yourself, if not for me and mom and dad, then for your niece or nephew."

His gaze penetrates me for a moment longer before he walks away and into the house, leaving me to ponder everything he's said. I'm going to be an aunt. *Holy hell, what if it's a girl?* I think back to my childhood, how close I was with my aunts and uncles, how much I looked up to them. I still do. *What if this child looks up to me and all I have to offer is who I am now?*

When Mom hollers that dinner's ready, I trudge inside and quietly sit through the meal as my thoughts whirl around at breakneck speed. Elijah and I share secret looks and sly smiles. I won't share his secret, although it's tempting because it would get the focus off of me. It would give my parents something else to fret about, something happy to expend their energy on. But it's not my information to divulge, so I don't.

Dinner ends and I leave, promising my family that I'll be back next week. I drive home but take a different route, one that's longer and gives me more time to think, to worry. When I pull in my driveway, I glance at Jett's house rather than my own.

There's a light glowing on the first floor, and rather than feel scared, I feel determined, excited... nervous. But no fear.

Before I can change my mind, I climb out of the car and march to his front door. I knock and step back, waiting for him to answer. The porch light comes on, and the door swings open.

"Emma? What are you doing here?" Jett's eyes convey a mixture of confusion and pleasure.

My mouth goes dry, and I wrap my arms around myself, trying to contain the anxiety that threatens to fly out of me. I lick my lips and peer at him, forcing courage to take over.

"Can I come in?"

12

JETT

The last thing I expected to happen was for Emma to show up on my doorstep. We haven't talked since she kicked me out of her house three weeks ago. I called and texted, hoping for even a sliver of communication. Radio silence. Until now.

"Yeah, sure." I step aside to let her pass. "Come on in."

She doesn't immediately enter, but after a few minutes of awkward staring, she breezes by me and plops down on the couch. I shut the door but don't flip the lock. I don't want her to feel like she's trapped. I shake my head and walk through the living room to the kitchen.

"Can I get you something to drink," I ask as I pass.

"Got any Tequila?"

I stop in my tracks and turn to retrace my steps to stand in front of her.

"That kind of visit, huh?"

She gives a curt nod and bites her bottom lip. My dick instantly hardens, and I swallow down a groan and remind myself that she's not here for that. She doesn't seem to notice my discomfort, thank God.

"No Tequila, but I do have Whiskey. That okay?"

She sighs, loudly, as if I crushed all of her hopes and dreams. I chuckle at her reaction, and she narrows her eyes at me. "I suppose it'll have to be, although Whiskey and I don't mix well." She wrinkles her nose, and it's cute as hell.

"I won't let you drink too much. Promise."

I leave her there and go to pour our drinks. I add a little extra Whiskey into her tumbler, not because I want her drunk but because she seems to need the fortification. I don't drink much, so my glass only has a splash in it, but it's enough.

When I return to the living room, Emma's not on the couch. She's standing in front of the TV, which hangs on the wall. Curious as to why she's staring at it, I take a step toward her and realize she's not looking at the TV, she's holding a picture-frame in her hands, the one that sits on the shelf below the TV, the only one I have.

She stiffens when I close the distance between us and hand her the Whiskey. She replaces the frame and turns to face me fully.

"He looks like you." She lifts the glass to her lips, takes a tentative sip. "Your brother."

"I look like him." When she quirks a brow, I explain. "Harrison is, *was*, my older brother. So I look like him."

"Right." She retreats to the couch and holds her glass in both hands, as if keeping a strong grip on it will make whatever she has to say easier.

I sit down next to her and smile to myself when she doesn't move. She's tense, yes, but not scared. Interesting.

"So, what brings you here, Emma? I wasn't sure if I was ever going to hear from you again."

She winces at the statement and hangs her head. "I wasn't sure you would either."

"What changed?"

"Honestly?" She shifts to face me, pulling a leg under her. "I'm gonna be an aunt. And I have no idea how to do that."

"And you thought I would?" I teasingly ask.

She glares at me, and I school my features. In that moment, with that look, I'm reminded of the prison guard she was and not the timid woman she's become.

"Be serious," she demands and takes a gulp of the amber liquid. "I look up to my aunts and have always considered them role models. I'm a horrible role model!"

"I doubt that, but I'm curious, what does that have to do with whether or not we see each other again?" If I was stunned by her standing on the other side of my door, this conversation takes that to a new level and adds a dose of confusion to the mix.

"I'm getting to that," she downs the rest of her Whiskey and leans forward to set it on the coffee table. When she sits back, she squares her shoulders and takes a deep breath. "As far back as I can remember, I wanted to work in the criminal justice system. Growing up, I was addicted to all the crime dramas and always fantasized about doing my part to make the system a little bit better. My family hated my career choice, but they supported me."

"Why did they hate it?" I ask when she pauses.

"I guess hate is a strong word. They worried about it, worried that I couldn't handle the *roughness* of it." Her eyes took on a pleading quality. "No offense."

"None taken. There's nothing easy about prison, whether as an inmate or as an employee. I don't blame them for the way they think."

"The thing is, they were right. I couldn't handle it." She drops her head, and when she raises it, there's a sheen in her eyes. "I'd been trained on how to handle a riot. I knew exactly what I was supposed to do, but in real life, nothing happened the way the textbooks said. They don't teach you how to deal with the aftermath of it. Don't get me wrong, there are trainings and conferences on how to deal with trauma, but it doesn't quite prepare you for when reality comes crashing in."

She's right. I've been to those conferences, participated in the trainings, and *nothing* prepares you for what actually happens.

"Afterward, I tried. I really did, but just stepping through my front door became too hard. I was always terrified that something bad would happen, that the world would swallow me up. One by one, my friends disappeared. My parents and brother acted funny when I was around. I never went back to work, not at the prison. Therapy didn't help."

I want to reach out to her, touch her, comfort her. But I'm terrified that it'll shatter the moment, so I busy my hands with my glass, which I'm wishing wasn't empty. Listening to her talk about her perceived failures, her weaknesses, breaks my heart and makes me itch to make it all better.

"When Elijah told me I'm going to be an aunt, he said something that got me thinking." She leans her elbow on the back of the couch, resting her head on her hand to prop herself up. "He said that his child is going to need me. God, Jett, those words? They did something that nothing in a year and a half has been able to do." She fists her free hand and presses it to her chest, her heart.

"What's that?" I hope like hell it's something good.

"Made me realize that I need to get a grip. I need to work through what happened and try this whole 'living life' thing again." Color tinges her cheeks a rosy pink, and the blush causes an unfamiliar emotion to surge through me.

"Yeah? That's great."

"It is. I think." Her gaze seems to unfocus, and she appears to be looking past me before bolstering herself and returning her eyes to mine. "But I need your help."

And once again, she's managed to shock the hell out of me. "Why?" I ask, uncertain, and then rush to add, "Not that I mind. I don't. I just… why me?"

"You were there." She lifts a shoulder, lets it fall. "My brother and Sierra are right. You're the one person who might understand what I went through."

"More than you know," I mumble.

"What?"

"Nothing." I shake my head to refocus and paste a smile on my face. "What can I do to help?"

"Well, I don't actually know." Her shoulders sag.

"Why don't we just take it a day at a time?" I suggest, recognizing this for the opportunity it is. "Something tells me that just spending time with me is difficult." I hold my hand up to stop her from interrupting. "It's okay, Emma. I get it. But we'll start with that and build from there."

"Build to what?" she asks, suspiciously.

"Relax." I reach out and rest a hand on her knee. She stares at it with narrowed eyes but doesn't flinch or pull away. "Just think of me as a life coach, of sorts."

She snorts. "A life coach that has a felony record and just got out of the slammer." She slaps a hand over her mouth, and her eyes grow wide. She pulls her hand away slightly. "I'm sorry. That was—"

"It's fine. But not entirely true." She's showing the first signs of the Emma I knew since seeing her again, and I like it. Like her. But I know that as far as the truth goes, it's now or never. "I need to tell you something."

She pulls away from me and fidgets with her hands in her lap. "Okay."

I take a deep breath and lean back against the cushions. "I'm not who you think I am."

Emma shoots up from the couch and tries to walk away, but I grab her hand and pull her back. "Hear me out," I plead when she's facing me again. She shakes her head back and forth but doesn't say anything. "Please?"

She glares at my grip on her hand, and I release her. Several moments pass before she sits back down. "Fine," she huffs out.

"Thank you." I search for the right words to say because even though my true identity isn't a bad thing, the fact that I've not told her yet is. "I know you think that I'm just like every other inmate you've come across, but I'm not."

"That's not exactly a revelation. If you were, I wouldn't have made it out of there. I wouldn't be here now."

"No, that's not what I mean. Not really." I swallow past the cotton that seems to coat my mouth. "I was undercover." Her eyes widen and then narrow slightly. "I was a DEA agent helping out the FBI try to get more information on Jeffrey Lee."

At the mention of Lee, the man who attacked her, Emma appears to shrink into herself.

"I'm not a bad guy. I'm one of the good ones. And I'm sorry I lied to you. Back then, I didn't have a choice, and recently, well, I didn't know how to tell you. But if I'm going to help you, you should know."

I slam my mouth closed when I realize I'm rambling. Emma sits quietly, seeming to digest the information. She maintains her focus on me, as if studying me, which is uncomfortable, but I say nothing. Let her study, let her examine.

Suddenly, she nods. "Okay."

"Okay?"

"Yes, okay." She sighs. "Knowing the truth doesn't really change anything other than you aren't actually a criminal. That doesn't erase what happened to me, it doesn't lessen my fear, it just... doesn't. What it does change is my earlier statement."

"Uh, which statement?"

"The one about a felon as a life coach." She doesn't smile, but there's a teasing quality to her voice. "The sentiment still stands, I guess. Just not the felon part."

"I still think I can help you, if you'll let me. But know this… I'm gonna push, demand more from you than you think you can give."

Fear enters her expression, and I rush to explain.

"Not like that. I mean, I'm not going to sit by and let you waste away in that house of yours." I nod to indicate the walls she hides behind. "It's not going to be easy, but I do think it'll be worth it. If you'll give me the chance."

I hold my breath for what feels like hours, silently waiting for her to find fault with what I have to offer. From the moment I carried her out of hell, I was lost. I never in a million years would have dreamed I'd have a chance to show her who I am, who I want to be, but here we are.

And as worried as I am that she won't agree, I think I'm more terrified that she will. Because then I have a chance to win her over, and it could backfire. She may not see me as anything other than the guy who saved her and lied to her, the guy who holds a piece of her past but has no place in her future.

"I'm in."

13

EMMA

"You okay over there?"

My palms are sweaty, my stomach is in knots, and I'm pretty sure I'm going to throw up, so no, I am not okay.

"Peachy," I say instead as I rub my hands up and down my thighs.

Jett chuckles at my half-hearted response and keeps his attention on the road. We're going grocery shopping, which for some people, that might be a simple task that life requires, but for me, it's torture. At least this time. Normally, I go to the same supermarket, no exceptions. I do that because it keeps my anxiety to a minimum, and it's the same one I've been going to my entire life so it feels safer than others.

Today, however, Jett insisted that we go to a grocery store that I've never been to before. I tried to get out of it. I complained of being sick, told him I had a fever. It would have worked, too, if he hadn't been such a damn decent guy and came over to check on me. He took one look at me and declared me 'just fucking fine' and now I'm sitting in his

Impala wondering how the hell I could ever have thought him decent.

"I told you I was going to push, that this wouldn't be easy," he reminds me.

"Yeah, well, yay for you."

Jett remains quiet, and I glance at him out of the corner of my eye. He's sporting a smile, and I'm torn between wanting to reach out and smack it off of his smug face and a sudden urge to trace the indentation of his dimple with a fingertip. I let my eyes roam down his body and take in the ink that peeks out from the sleeve of his T-shirt. My mouth goes dry when I see his thigh bunching beneath his jeans as he shifts his foot from the gas pedal to the brake.

I try to remember that I asked him for this, that I wanted to rejoin the land of the living, but it's difficult. I should have asked Sierra to help me. At least with her, I wouldn't have the added frustration of attraction. I'm damaged, not dead, after all.

"Are we almost there?" I ask, the words sounding breathless.

"Almost."

I avert my stare when he looks at me, hoping like hell that he can't tell what I'm thinking. He glances between me and the road in front of us, and there are questions in his eyes. Questions I definitely don't want to answer.

When Jett showed up to check on me, I took one look at him and my entire body tingled. And not from shock or anger that he didn't believe me when I said I was sick. Jett is sex personified, and as much as I try to ignore my attraction to him, it's always there, tempting me, taunting me. Problem with that is I can't act on it. It's been over two years since I last had sex, and while I enjoyed it, I somehow know that anything I've experienced before won't come close to what Jett could do.

"Define 'almost,'" I demand, frustration clear. I tap my foot on the floorboard, anything to keep my body focused on something other than his incredible sex appeal.

"You are fucking adorable all riled up, ya know that?" He quirks his brow at me before adjusting his grip on the steering wheel and shifting in his seat.

My gaze snaps to his face, and my tapping stops. I huff out a breath and the heat that infuses my cheeks is embarrassing. "Just drive."

"I'm trying to, doll, but you're making it difficult."

Jett flips on his turn signal and pulls into the parking lot. We have arrived, and suddenly, all of my anxiety returns. My eyes dart around the parking lot to take in all of the cars. It's crowded, more so than one would expect in the middle of the week. When he parks the car, I strain to see around me, past the trucks he pulls in between.

"Ready?" he asks once he shuts off the engine.

I shake my head, a lump in my throat making it impossible to talk.

"Sure you are." He exits the vehicle and walks around to open my door.

When I make no move to get out, he reaches in and holds out his hand.

"C'mon. I'll be right beside you the whole time. There's nothing to be afraid of."

I stare at his hand for a moment longer before taking it and allowing him to tug me out. His hand engulfs my much smaller one, and I let the warmth of it, the security of it, seep into my bones. My eyes slide closed, and I focus on Jett, his smell, his touch. While I'm standing there, a hand cups my cheek and I lean into it, taking everything it has to offer.

"You are so goddamn beautiful." Jett's voice is deep, husky.

My eyes snap open, and the spark in his catches me off

guard. For a moment, I forget we're in a parking lot. I forget that I'm terrified of being somewhere unfamiliar. I forget my freaking name.

"Let's get this over with," I whisper, needing to move, do something, anything that will take my mind off of him and what I can't have.

He laughs at me but tightens his hold on my hand and urges me toward the entrance. As we walk, all I see are dangers. The guy pushing his cart through the lot and leering at me, the alley next to the building, the yellow poles that stick out of the ground at the curb. Everything I see is a potential threat, and I grip Jett's hand like a lifeline.

"I've got you, doll."

His breath skitters across my neck as he speaks in my ear. A shiver races down my spine, and I shudder at the sensation.

Yeah. You sure do.

Something tells me I'm going to get more than I bargained for with this man.

~

The shopping trip is a success, despite me constantly looking over my shoulder and analyzing perceived threats and potential safety measures. Jett did as promised and never left my side. In fact, he never broke contact with me, keeping my hand in his, reassuring me throughout the entire afternoon.

"That's the last of it."

Jett drops the last grocery bag on the counter with a thud. He steps back and peers at my purchases before turning to study me. I feel like a withering flower under his stare, but he doesn't relent.

When I can't take his scrutiny any longer, I grab a bag and start putting things away. It isn't long before he's helping. We manage to get it done in record time, but each time we pass one another, our bodies touch, barely, and a zing ricochets through me. When everything is in its place, I'm practically panting like I've just run a marathon.

"Thanks again for today." I hand him a glass of water and sit on a stool.

"And to think, you tried to get out of it." He chuckles and stands on the other side of the island, elbows resting on the granite.

"Yeah, sorry about that." I duck my head, hoping to hide the evidence of his effect on me.

"Why do you do that?" he asks, and his fingertips graze my forehead as he brushes a strand of hair out of my face.

"Do what?"

"Look away from me? Hide from me?" His touch trails to my chin and lifts it up so I have no choice but to gaze into his eyes.

I bite the inside of my cheek, not sure how to answer his questions. I do hide from him. To be fair, I hide from everybody, but for far different reasons. He makes me come alive inside when I've been dead for so long.

"Emma?"

"Hmm?"

"If we're going to be spending time together, how much longer do you plan to fight yourself?" He cocks his head and lets his hand fall.

That's an excellent question. One that raises a few of my own. Is he attracted to me? Is he helping me because he wants more? If he is, do I care?

I want out of this new prison I've created, and he's ready and willing to help me so I might as well take all he has to offer. Right?

"What would happen if I stopped fighting?"

I pull my bottom lip between my teeth when his eyes

widen. His nostrils flare, and his shoulders tense. Just when I think I've said the wrong thing, a grin tugs at the corners of his mouth.

"Anything you want, doll." He leans across the counter and cups my cheek. "And so much more than you're prepared for."

His lips capture mine, and his tongue glides along their seam. My instinct is to push him away, deny him access, but it feels so damn good. I plant my palms on the granite and leverage myself up and closer to him. I let his tongue in, let it tangle with mine. The kiss intensifies, and sparks dance across my skin, branding me with the feel of him, the taste of him.

He breaks the kiss and pulls his head back to look at me. I whimper at the loss of contact, which only causes him to groan. His green eyes are dark and full of need.

"Why'd you stop?"

"Because I don't think you have a fucking clue what you're doing to me. What you've done to me since the first time I laid eyes on you." He quirks a brow at what he's suggesting, daring me to contradict him.

I fall back onto the stool and look away. He comes around the counter and stands behind me. His hands rub up and down my arms, raising goosebumps across my flesh.

"Jett, I…"

"What do you want, doll? Tell me," He whispers in my ear. He captures my lobe between his lips and sucks, eliciting sensations that I haven't felt in a long time. Maybe never.

"Mmmm. I, um, I can't think when you're…" I lose my train of thought when he bites down. I groan when pleasure turns to pain and pain turns to pleasure.

"Don't think," he growls. "Just feel."

His hands move from my arms to my hips, and he urges me off of the stool. I try and turn, but he doesn't let me. The stool scrapes across the floor as he shoves it out of his way and steps close, pressing his erection into me.

"Feel that?" When I nod, he continues. "That's what you do to me. That's what I deal with every time I look at you. Every time I think about you."

I swallow past the lump in my throat. How is it possible that someone like him would want someone like me? I'm damaged and he's perfection.

His hands move from my hips to the hem of my shirt, and he lifts it up, exposing my back. He runs his fingertips from the top of my jeans to my bra, where he quickly opens the clasp. He replaces his fingertips with his lips, and he trails kisses along my spine, down to my waist. My vision blurs and my body tingles.

Without thinking, I reach down and tear my shirt over my head, tossing it to the floor. I hear his breath hitch, and my heart thunders against my ribs. Every single one of my nerve endings are on fire, and he's the only one that can douse the flames. He slides my bra straps off my shoulders and spins me around.

"Don't," he pleads when I raise my hands to cover myself.

I drop my arms and try to regulate my breathing. His gaze goes from my eyes to my lips and then it dips lower. My nipples pebble under his stare, and he smiles.

"Fucking beautiful."

He lifts me in his palms and lowers his head to suck a nipple into his mouth, swirling his tongue around it. My legs tremble, and just when I think I'm going to collapse, he picks me up and sets me on the counter. He steps between my legs as he rips his shirt off.

My mouth goes dry. I've seen him without a shirt before but never this close. His muscles are bunching, and his tattoos appear to dance across his body. I reach out and place my hands on his chest, tentatively. I'm shaking and I have no doubt he sees it, feels it in my touch.

"Are you scared?" he asks as he places a hand over one of mine, holding me to him. I nod, incapable of speech. "Of what?"

It takes me a minute to come up with an answer. Not because I don't know what the answer is but because I'm so enthralled with *him* that forcing the words out is damn near impossible.

"So many things," I finally say.

"Like?"

He kneads my breasts as he waits, but his eyes never leave mine. It's erotic and intimate and fucking terrifying.

"It's been so long since…"

He stiffens and takes a step back but he still doesn't look away. "How long?" I shrug and he shakes his head as if to elicit a better answer. "How. Long?"

I take a few deep breaths, trying to calm my racing heart. Only now, it's racing because of shame and embarrassment, not lust, not need or desire.

"Since before the riot," I whisper.

14

JETT

Since before the riot.

Emma's words are echoing in my head. I know I should say something, do something. Instead, I'm standing here, frozen, because I finally have her right where I want her and I'm not sure I can do this the way she deserves.

"Jett?" Her voice is quiet, barely above a whisper.

My gaze snaps to hers, and I swallow past the lump in my throat when I see a tear slide down her cheek. I reach out to brush it away, and she squeezes her eyes shut.

"Aw, Em," I say as I cup her cheek. "Why are you crying? I can handle a lot of things, but seeing you cry isn't one of them."

"I don't even know." She opens her eyes and peers at me.

"What else are you afraid of? You said there are 'so many things'."

She takes a deep breath and averts her gaze. "What if I can't… you know?"

"What if you can?" Her head snaps back, and she stares at me, wide-eyed, like she hasn't even considered that thought. "There's no denying that you were traumatized and you've dealt with it in your own way. But that doesn't make it the only way or the best way."

I want her, there's no denying that, but she's not ready. As much as it kills me, I bend over and pick up her shirt.

"What are you doing?" She looks confused, hurt.

"I'm making an executive decision." I hand her the top, and when she doesn't take it, I pull it over her head and help guide her arms through the sleeves. "You aren't ready for this, and there's nothing wrong with that."

"But... I thought you wanted this. Wanted me."

"Oh, I want you, doll. So goddamn bad, but now isn't the right time."

She hops off the counter and starts to pace. After a few passes of the room, she stops in front of me and pokes a finger into my chest.

"I want this. You told me you would help me with this, and now you're giving up."

"Emma, when we have sex, it's not going to be because you're forcing yourself to do it. It'll be because you want it so bad that nothing else matters." I rest my hands on her shoulders and bend at the knees so I'm eye level with her. "It's gonna happen, trust me on that. But you're not just some fucking notch on my bedpost."

She blinks rapidly, seemingly trying to understand what I'm saying. Trying to determine if I'm being honest or not. I am. She means too much to me to treat her like some two-dollar whore that I can bang and then forget about. And if we fucked now, that's exactly how I'd be treating her.

"If we're not going to have sex, what are we going to do?"

"I dunno." I straighten and shrug. "Honestly, I don't care. I just like spending time with you."

She wrinkles her nose and glances around the room. When her gaze lands back on me, she huffs out a breath.

"If we're not gonna have sex than you're going to have to

put your shirt back on. You're too tempting." With that, she walks out of the kitchen and into the living room.

I chuckle at her honesty. She might think she's some timid victim, but she's not. Not always. Sure, she's closed herself off from the world, she's missed out on so much because of fear, but I still see her fighting spirit, hints of the woman I knew, even if it was mostly in passing while I was in the cage.

~

Sitting here, Emma's head resting on my shoulder as she sleeps, I begin to wonder if I'm a glutton for punishment. I already had a case of blue balls when we sat down to watch the movie, and it hasn't improved over the last two hours.

The credits are rolling on the television screen. I know I should wake her up, if for no other reason than her neck is going to be killing her. During the movie she inched her way closer to me, and eventually we were touching. When she fell asleep, I couldn't stop the elation at the fact that she trusts me enough to do so, whether she realizes it or not.

I try to stand without waking her, and when she starts mumbling, I freeze. I hold my breath when I try again and as I do, I make sure to hold her head and guide it to the couch so she can lay flat. When her head hits the cushion, she rolls over and curls in on herself. I cover her with the throw hanging on the back of the sofa before bending over and placing a kiss on the top of her head.

"Sleep tight, doll," I whisper.

I make sure that everything that should be off is and then head out the front door, locking it. When I step out onto the porch, I breathe in the crisp air. It's not late, but the sun has started to set, and the sky is a brilliant mixture of orange and red.

I jog down her steps and, out of habit, glance up and down the street. I had to look over my shoulder for so long and that's one thing that I haven't been able to break myself of. I notice a car parked a few houses down, and something about it has the hairs on my neck standing up. The headlights are on but are quickly dimmed when I look in that direction. I can't see anyone in the vehicle at this distance, but clearly there's someone in the car.

I want to take off down the street and find out why this particular vehicle has all my senses tingling but know that if I do that, I won't get answers. But a man walking a dog just might. I look up to the sky, pretending that I'm not buzzing with suspicion and then head to my place to get Freedom.

She's happy to see me and goes a little crazy when I grab her leash. I get her all hooked up, and when we step onto the porch, I immediately look toward the car. It's gone. Freedom pulls me down the steps and goes in the direction I planned. I look over my shoulder and back in front of me, sure that I'm missing something, that the car still has to be there.

There's nothing, and for a minute, I wonder if I'm losing my mind. So there was a car parked on the street that I didn't recognize. So what? It was probably an Uber or someone picking up a friend. Nothing wrong with that.

I don't believe that though. I can't put a finger on why, but it feels *off*. My days as a DEA agent and undercover in a prison made me paranoid. That's all it is.

Freedom and I finish our walk, and once we're back inside, I make sure she has food and water and head to the shower. I don't really need one, but just thinking about jail makes me feel dirty.

As I step under the spray, water sluices down my body, and almost immediately, the suspicious car is forgotten and an image of Emma enters my mind. She's sitting on her kitchen counter, almost exactly like she was mere hours earlier, only in my head, she's completely naked, and her legs are spread so that her throbbing sex is wide open for me.

My cock jumps at the flashing images, and I brace a hand on the shower wall while I fist my dick with the other. I picture Emma throwing her head back while I bend and suck her clit between my lips, nipping at the bundle of nerves. Her moans of ecstasy have me groaning, and I tighten my grip, pumping furiously to chase the release my body craves.

When the scene morphs to Emma bending over the counter and my dick being swallowed up by her pussy, the tingling begins and my balls draw tight. I increase my speed, and my hand mimics the pressure of her walls milking me as she comes.

My body stiffens, and I shout out my orgasm. If just fantasizing about her is this good, then I can only assume that the real thing will be life altering, soul shattering, incredible beyond expectation. I just hope I can make it that good for her.

After washing my hair, I step out and wrap a towel around my waist. I sift through my drawers until I find a pair of sweats and slip those on. I make my way downstairs and notice that Emma's lights are all on when I pass the window. She must not have slept very long.

I grab a beer from the fridge and flop down on the couch and switch the TV on. As I scroll through the channels, I think back over my original plan to contact Emma's best friend, Sierra, for information. I didn't follow through with it because Emma asked me for help on her own and it didn't seem necessary, but now I wonder. Should I call her? I quickly discard the idea as too sneaky. I want Emma to trust me, not feel like I'm going behind her back.

After watching a few hours of mindless television, my eyes grow heavy with exhaustion and I decide to go to bed. When I lock the front door, I spot the car from earlier parked outside, but when I throw my door open to go get some answers, whoever is in it takes off and I'm left wondering, again.

I glance toward Emma's house, and most of her lights are now off, other than the one in her bedroom. I see her shadow through the curtain, and I find myself staring, wishing I was up there with her. I shake my head and force myself to look away and go inside.

I lock up again and trudge up the stairs. I crawl into bed, and it isn't more than a few minutes before the sound of Freedom padding across the floor to her doggy bed reaches my ears. I sit up and watch as she does circle after circle, trying to find just the right spot, and plops down, heaving a loud sigh as she does, as if expelling the weight of the world from her body so she can relax.

I drop back down to the bed, and my mind races. I stare at the ceiling and think about that damn car. I think about how I almost got to feel what it was like to have Emma wrapped around my body. I think about my life and wonder if I can trust the happiness that's seeping its way into my existence.

My last thought before sleep takes over is that I do deserve to be happy but that with my luck, the proverbial other shoe will no doubt drop soon.

15

EMMA

Just do it already.

I'm staring at my phone, my thumbs hovering over the keyboard in the texting app, having an internal debate with myself about whether or not I should text Jett. As bad as I want to, I can't help but remember that I woke up yesterday evening and he was gone.

I didn't mean to fall asleep during the movie, but I was exhausted. Grocery shopping had taken its toll and add in the other *activities* of the day and I'd been wiped.

There were no other activities. It stopped before it could really get started.

Groaning, I toss my phone down on the bed and go in search of coffee. Maybe a little caffeine will make me a bit more decisive. As I step off the last stair, something catches my eye on the floor.

I pick up the small piece of lined paper and unfold it. As I read the words, the corners of my mouth lift into a smile.

I'm having fun. Miss you.

I hold the paper to my chest and rush up the steps to get

my phone. Screw coffee. I'm texting Jett. When I reach the bed, I throw myself down like a schoolgirl waiting on a phone call from her crush. It's pathetic, really, but I don't care. Jett might be a reminder of what I suffered, but he also makes me remember that I survived.

Me: Having fun 2. If u miss me u should come over

I stare at the words, my brain throwing all the reasons I shouldn't hit send into the forefront of my thoughts. Before I can change my mind, or let my brain win, I hit the button and the words are sent with a whoosh.

Now that I can't take them back, I race to the shower and get myself presentable, just in case he decides to follow through. When I'm dressed, hair and make-up done, I force myself to leisurely drink my morning coffee and not check my phone every ten seconds to see if he responded or stand by the door and wait for his knock.

At 9:06am, the knock finally comes. I chastise myself for knowing the exact time because that means I failed at not constantly looking at my cell. As I walk to the door, I smooth my hands down my thighs, hoping to rid them of the sweat.

When I open the door and see Jett standing there, it takes me a minute to realize he's not alone. He's got his dog with him.

"Mornin'." His smile is wide and genuine as he lifts the leash. "Thought you might want to walk with us."

"I, uh…" I lean through the doorway, glance up and down the street and then return my gaze to Jett. My palms are sweaty again, my stomach in knots, and I'm not sure if it's the man or the thought of leaving the house. I look at Freedom, her pink tongue lolling out the side of her mouth and her eyes pleading with me to say yes. "Sure, why not?"

I grab my keys off the hook by the door and pocket them before I step over the threshold and pull the door closed behind me. I test the knob to make sure it's locked and, satisfied that no one can get in while I'm gone, I give Jett a tentative smile.

"We won't go far, I promise," he says as he links his hand with mine and we walk down the steps.

"I trust you." The moment the words leave my mouth, I know they're true. I do trust Jett. When that happened, I'm not quite sure, but it probably started the day of the riot.

We walk slowly, and Freedom remains patient with us. It's clear that she wants to run, but she doesn't pull away or try to get ahead. Jett really has done a great job with her. *He's done a great job with you.* We're mostly silent, only speaking when necessary, but it doesn't feel strained or awkward. It feels right.

"Your note was very sweet," I say when we're back at my door and I've got the key in the lock.

"What note?" Jett asks, confusion swimming in his eyes.

"The note you slid under my door." My eyes narrow as the words pass my lips. "I'm sorry I didn't see it last night. I was exhausted and must have just missed it when I went to bed."

Jett's expression goes from confused to pissed off so fast I'm left to wonder if I'm imagining things. He pushes my hand out of the way and twists the key to unlock the door. When he hears the click, he throws the door open, and it bangs into the wall.

"Jett, what are you doing? You're scaring me." My legs tremble and my head starts to spin.

"Here, hold on to Freedom and stay out here on the porch." He thrusts the leash into my hand and forces my fingers to wrap around the braided nylon loop. He leans down and kisses me, hard and fast. "I'll be right back, doll."

And then he's gone. Into the house like a mad man, and I have no idea why. I sit on one of the rocking chairs, and Freedom lays over my feet, head on her paws, like she doesn't have a care in the world. I stroke her fur and murmur to her, even though she can't hear me.

I can hear Jett stomping through the house, shouting at whatever or whoever he thinks might be inside. After a few minutes, he comes back out and joins me on the porch. He kneels in front of me and braces his hands on my knees.

Staring at him, seeing the concern, the anger, in his emerald eyes, a thought barrels into me. I'm not worried. I'm not shaking or nauseous or scared. I was before he took off into my house, clearly thinking there was a threat, but knowing he was handling it made the fear slip away. I'm just sitting on the porch, calm as can be. Confident that he'll ensure my safety.

"Holy shit," I mumble.

Jett arches a brow and cocks his head. "What?"

"I'm not afraid." My lips pull into a grin. "You went in there like a bat outta hell, and I'm not scared. I mean, at first I was, but then…"

"Then what?" he asks as he traces circles over my kneecaps with his thumb.

"I don't know." I shrug. "I just wasn't anymore. I sat down with Freedom and listened to you yell through the house, and I just knew if something was wrong, you'd take care of it."

"Yeah?"

I nod and stand up, pulling him up with me. I still have the leash in my hand, and Freedom is now dancing around our feet, but I lean into Jett and wrap my arms around his waist and lay my head against his chest. His heart is hammering, and I savor the feel of it throbbing on my cheek.

Jett heaves a sigh and urges me away from him, his hands around my upper arms. His smile is sad, and immediately, my sense of happy calm begins to diminish.

"What?" I ask.

"I hate that you trust me and you're happy and not scared and I'm going to ruin it."

"I don't understand." I shake my head. "Why are you going to ruin it?"

"Emma," he pauses, inhales deeply. "I didn't leave you a note."

My stomach plummets to the floor. I stare at him, silently pleading for him to take the words back, tell me he's joking. He does none of those things. I yank away from him and rush inside, trying to slam the door behind me. Jett stops it from shutting it in his face and follows me upstairs and into my bedroom.

I throw open my closet door and drop to my knees in front of the safe. Jett stands over my shoulder, watching my every move, concern creasing his forehead.

"What are you doing?"

"Protecting myself," I snap. I twist the dial, first left, then right and then left again. The steel door pops open, and my Glock 26 is there, right where I put it so I wouldn't use it on myself. Out of sight, out of mind.

I reach out to pick it up, and when my fingertips graze the black grip, I yank my hand back as if burned. I take a deep breath and blow it out. When I touch the weapon again, I run my fingers over it as if introducing myself to an old friend. I pick it up and the weight of it in my palm is familiar, comforting.

"You've gotta be fucking kidding me." Jett stomps away and then returns to my side as I stand up. "The fuck you need that for?"

"Whoever put a note in my house and made me think it was you!" I yell.

"You don't need that." Jett tries to grab the Glock from me, and I spin away from him.

He tips his head back, and it sounds like he's counting to

ten. *Losing patience?* Maybe. Probably. When he reaches ten, he refocuses his attention on me and his body relaxes as he smiles.

"Emma, c'mon. You don't need that. There's no one in the house but you and me."

"You don't know that."

"I do. I checked every room." He cups my cheek, and I lean into his touch. "Let's just sit down and talk about this before you do something crazy."

"So now you think I'm crazy?" I pull away from him and storm out of the room and down the steps. I know I'm being irrational, but it's how I deal.

Jett's footsteps thud behind me, and he manages to get ahead of me and grip my arms to stop me from fleeing from him.

"I don't think you're crazy, woman," he snaps. "You're being a little infuriating right now, but you're not crazy."

I try to shove away from him, but he holds me immobile. His arms wrap around me, and his fingers span my lower back. When my body relaxes in his embrace, he begins to loosen his hold, and his hands move up my spine to cup the back of my head.

I tip my head back and look into his eyes. What I see scares me but also turns me on. His green irises are dark, hungry. Heat pools in my belly and without realizing what I'm doing, I run my hands up under his shirt and dig my nails into his pecs.

"What are you doing to me?" he growls a second before his lips fuse to mine.

16

JETT

"I wish I had better news."

Slade's voice is tinged with regret, and I hurl my coffee mug at the wall. Glass shatters and brown liquid runs down the white paint to pool at the floor. I shove my fingers through my hair and tug on the strands in agitated frustration.

"How the hell am I supposed to protect her if I don't know what I'm protecting her from?"

"Is that what you want? To protect Emma?"

"What choice do I have?"

"There's always a choice," Slade responds patiently. "You're not an agent anymore. It's not your job to make sure she's safe. Besides, it's not likely that the note is even related to Lee or anyone else you dealt with while in the DEA."

"True, but..."

Silence hangs in the air after my words trail off. What if Slade's wrong? What if it is related to Lee? And what if my need to protect her has nothing to do with a sense of duty and everything to do with my growing feelings for her?

"Listen, Jett," Slade begins. "I know we don't know each

other very well, but if you want my honest opinion, I'll give it to you."

I consider his words and decide that I do want his opinion… both personally and professionally.

"Lay it on me."

"Okay. You've got a few options. You can walk away from whatever there is between the two of you and no one would blame you. You barely know her, and she's not your responsibility. Another option is to keep seeing her and stay alert. You're more than capable of protecting her. Or you can continue to see her and pretend like your spidey senses aren't tingling."

"That's not exactly advice, Slade. Those are options. Which would you choose?"

"Me?" He chuckles. "I'd stick with her and take things as they come."

"That's what I was afraid of."

"Look, you can't stop feeling whatever it is you're feeling. But you can decide how you want to deal with it. I'm guessing Emma's a pretty smart cookie. Why don't you explain your concerns to her, both for her safety and your feelings? Let her be the deciding factor?"

"Yeah, that's probably what I'll do." I plop down on a kitchen chair. "So, you really weren't able to find anything?"

"Jett, you didn't give me much to work with," he says. "I wasn't able to find any vehicles linked to Lee or known associates that match the one you described. As for the note, it's being checked for fingerprints, but I doubt we'll get anything."

"Right."

"Is there anyone else that you can think of that might not like Emma? Did she give you any names or clues as to who might want to scare her?"

"No. The only person I can think of is Len Harden, the doc at the prison. But she swears he's not a threat."

"Clearly you don't agree. What made you think of him?"

"He just always rubbed me the wrong way. While I was undercover, I actually thought he and Lee were connected somehow, but I never could link them. And during the riot, he did nothing to help Emma. She says it's because he's a pussy and that he's harmless. She also said that he had a crush on her, but he stopped trying to contact her not long after she quit her job."

"Why do you think this Len guy was linked to Lee? I don't recall that being in any of your reports."

"I didn't put it in because there wasn't anything specific. Just a gut feeling."

"I always say trust your gut. I'll do some checking into him and see what I can come up with. If there's nothing, no harm done, but if there's something, I'd rather know about it."

"Let me know what you find out?"

"I will. In the meantime, do whatever feels right. If that's being with Emma, that's fine. Just be careful."

I end the call with Slade, and while I clean up my coffee mess, I go back over our conversation. I hate that Emma may be in danger, but I'm not going to let that stop me from spending time with her.

I make the decision to get her some security equipment. I'm rather surprised she hasn't done that already, but who am I to judge?

∽

"She's not home."

I whirl around at the sound of the familiar voice and immediately recognize Emma's friend, Sierra. She's wearing a black pantsuit, and it's impossible to deny that she's beautiful, but she doesn't hold a candle to Emma.

"Oh. I, uh... any idea when—"

"What's in the bags?" she asks nodding toward the purchases in my hand.

"You first," I counter, tipping my head toward the plastic bags dangling from her fingers.

"Dinner." Sierra flashes a smile. "Your turn."

"I noticed that Emma doesn't have any cameras or motion sensor lights or any security equipment." I shrug. "Seemed odd for someone who doesn't like the outside world."

"So you got her those things? Equipment to make her feel safe?"

Nerves begin to attack me from the inside out, and I'm suddenly second-guessing my decision. Am I overstepping? What if Emma doesn't have these things for a reason?

"I just thought I might be able to help." My tone has a bite to it, a defensiveness that I can't mask.

"I'm sorry," Sierra says quickly. "I wasn't judging. It's just..."

"Just what?"

"It's sweet. She needs someone like you. Someone who will make her feel safe, who will make her want to return to the land of the living."

I can't help the laugh that escapes, but when she narrows her eyes at me, I quickly stop and school my features. I didn't mean to offend her, but it seems that may be what I did.

"Sorry, didn't mean to laugh," I say apologetically. "Do you know when she'll be home?"

"Should be any minute. She went to her brother's for a bit, but last I talked to her, she was on her way." Sierra glances at her watch and her brows furrow. "Hmm..."

"What?" I snap when I notice the worry on her face.

"Nothing, it's just..." She looks up and purses her lips

before taking a deep breath and continuing. "She should be here by now, that's all. Maybe she stopped at the store or something."

She doesn't sound convinced. Sierra looks up and down the road as if willing Emma to turn down it. My gut twists into knots, and I'm instantly on high alert. I pull out my cell phone and dial a number I memorized the first day I got it.

"You've reached Emma. I can't come to the phone right—"

"Dammit!" I end the call and shove my phone back in my pocket. "Here, take these."

I thrust my bags into Sierra's chest so she has no option but to take them and step around her to jog down the steps.

"Where are you going?" she shouts after me.

"I'm going to find Emma," I call over my shoulder. I get in my Impala and slam the door shut behind me. When I crank the engine, I roll the window down to yell at Sierra. "Get inside and lock the door. Don't open it for anyone unless it's Emma or me. If she shows up, have her call me."

I don't wait for a response as I pull out of my driveway and peel off down the street toward Emma's brother's house. I ignore the voice inside my head that reminds me that Emma never actually told me where her brother lives. I tracked down the information on my own. I know where all of her family lives. I know a lot about her that she doesn't know.

And it's the information I got for myself that is apparently going to keep her safe.

17

EMMA

Breathe, Em. Just breathe.

I repeat this mantra over and over and over again as I sit in the same spot I've been in for the last twenty minutes. I'm surrounded by vehicles with pissed off drivers who seem to be very inconvenienced by the stopped traffic.

I glance at my cell and silently curse myself for not getting a new car charger. Mine has been on it's last leg for a few months, but I kept putting off getting a new one because I rarely drive anywhere.

The brake lights in front of me disappear, and I shift my car into drive. Finally, we're getting somewhere. I let my foot off the brake and glide along behind the vehicles in front of me, but we only manage to make it a few feet before we're stopped again.

Sierra must be so worried. I should have been home by now, and I have no doubt she's waiting on me to get movie night started. The clock mocks me as the minutes tick by and my heartbeat slams against my ribs.

Breathe, Em. Just breathe.

I try to forget that I'm a sitting duck if someone wanted

to do me harm, but it's damn near impossible. Images of the riot flash before my eyes, and I break out into a clammy sweat. I rub my palms over my thighs and take a few deep breaths. My eyes slide closed, and my body slowly starts to relax.

My heart rate seems to reset, but it doesn't last long because a car horn blares behind me, startling me into irregularity again.

"Dammit," I mutter to myself as I look in the rearview mirror and see the guy behind me flipping me off.

I throw the car into gear and lurch forward to join the now moving traffic. A few hundred yards ahead I'm able to see what the holdup was. There's a car off the road, and it looks identical to mine.

There are no other signs of an accident, so I assume the majority of it was cleaned up while we sat and waited. The vehicle's front end is smashed in, and the tires on the driver's side appear to have blown. I slow my car and turn into a looky-loo as I scan the wooded area beyond the wrecked vehicle.

A man standing in the trees catches my eye, and I swerve to pull over and see if he's okay. Stupid? Probably. But the way he's looking around makes him seem like he's lost. Or maybe he was in the wrecked car and got thrown somehow. Who knows?

I turn off my engine and pull on the lever to open my door. Just as I'm about to step out, I hear the roar of an engine and my heart stops at the familiarity of it. I glance up in time to see a black Chevy Impala skid to a stop in front of me, facing the wrong direction.

I watch in fascination as Jett exits the Impala, and I can't stop the way I seem to shrink into myself at the angry expression on his face. He stomps toward me with rage in his eyes and tension rolling off of him in furious waves.

"What the hell are you doing?" Jett demands when he's a foot away from me.

I blink rapidly as I try to formulate an answer.

"Jesus, Emma." He takes another step closer and rests his hands on my shoulders, shaking me a little as he does. "Answer me."

"I..." I swallow past the lump in my throat. "I was getting out to help that guy."

I glance over my shoulder to point toward the man in the trees, but he's not there. I narrow my eyes, and my stomach twists into painful knots. When I look back at Jett, his narrowed eyes mirror my own.

"What guy, Emma? There's no one there."

"But..."

"Do you have any idea how fucking terrified I was when I saw that car on the side of the road, mangled almost beyond recognition?"

"I... no." I shake my head.

"Sierra's back at your place, scared out of her mind because you were late and you weren't answering your damn phone. So I came to look for you, and this is what I see." He points toward the smashed car.

"My phone's dead."

"What?" he snaps.

"My phone. It's dead." The longer Jett talks, the steadier I feel. My anger is rising, and he's going to be on the receiving end of it in a minute. "I'm sorry if that inconvenienced you, but it's not my fault. And as for the car, clearly it's not mine."

Jett lets out a bitter huff. "No, clearly it's not. But how was I supposed to know that?"

"I don't know," I concede.

Jett starts to pace between his vehicle and mine. I watch his expressions as they cross his features. Anger, frustration, relief, doubt, self-loathing, fear, more relief.

Relief?

"Jett?"

I reach out and place my hand on his forearm, stopping him in his tracks. He stares at where we're connected, and his eyebrows rise toward his hairline. After several tense seconds, he turns his attention to me and gazes into my eyes.

"I'm sorry I scared you." I mean the words. Even though I don't understand why he was scared or why he would worry about *me*, I *am* sorry.

"I'm not who you need to apologize to," he grits out. "Sierra is the one at your house waiting for you."

I pull my hand back at his words. There's a bite to his tone, and I'm not sure why.

"Okay. I'll apologize to her when I get home."

I turn around to get back in my car, and Jett's hand grips my bicep.

"I didn't mean to snap at you," he says to my back. I give a curt nod but make no move to rid myself of his touch. "Emma, please look at me."

When he drops his hand and it slaps against his thigh, I heave a sigh and turn around.

"What?" I cross my arms over my chest defensively.

"Are you okay?"

The look in his eyes soothes my frayed emotions, and I let my arms fall to my sides.

"I'm fine. I just…" I pause and look back toward the tree line. "I didn't like getting stuck in traffic. I felt too exposed. And then there was that guy and then you. It's just a lot to process for me. I know it wouldn't be for most people, but I'm not most people."

"No, you're not." He smiles, revealing perfectly straight white teeth. "You're better than most people."

I chuckle at him out of nervousness. "I doubt that."

"You don't believe me," he states matter-of-factly. "But you will. Someday."

"Maybe."

"You said you saw a man standing over there." He points toward where the man was, and the change in subject is a relief. "Did you see what he looked like? Any features or anything?"

I shake my head. "Nothing really. He just seemed lost or confused or something. I don't know."

"Want me to go check it out? See if I can find anything?"

The offer shocks me. I was expecting him to placate me, pretend that he believes me. I was definitely not expecting him to feed into my questionable sighting. Something about the man standing there tugs at me, and I can't shake it so I take him up on his offer.

"Yeah." I shut my car door. "But I'm coming with you."

I walk around to the passenger side of my vehicle and open the door. I reach in and grab my handgun from my purse. I check to be sure it's loaded, even though I know it is. Ever since I took it out of the safe, I'm never without it, loaded and ready to go.

Jett is already a few feet ahead of me into the grass along the highway. "Wait for me," I call after him.

Jett glances over his shoulder, and when he spots the weapon in my hand, he stops and turns around.

"What's that for?" He tilts his head toward the gun.

"Protection."

"From what?" He crosses his arms and his muscles bunch beneath the cotton of his T-shirt.

"I don't know. Whatever I might need protection from." There's no mistaking the challenge in my tone.

"You don't trust me to protect you?"

"That's not fair. You know I trust you."

"Do I?"

"You should," I snap. "You're the only person I've let into my life other than my family and Sierra since… well, since."

"Fair point." He reaches out and takes the gun from my hand. "You won't be needing this." He shoves it into his waistband at the small of his back. When his hand is free, he steps toward me and wraps an arm around my shoulders. "I've got you."

Yes. Yes, you do.

18

JETT

Emma tenses under the weight of my arm on her shoulders. I can't help the grin that forms, but I turn my face away so she can't see it. She's warming up to me, more than she's willing to admit and I'm loving every second of it.

"Um, so, what exactly are we looking for?"

I school my features and return my attention to her. "Anything really."

"Unicorns?" she counters with a salty bite to her tone.

I bark out a laugh and let go of her so I can face her fully. "No, smart ass." She smirks. "We're looking for anything that would point us in the right direction of the person you saw."

"You believe me?"

Sadness washes over me at the doubt in her words. "Of course I do," I assure her.

"Good."

"Keep an eye out for footprints or flattened leaves or patches of grass. Anything really that would—"

"Cigarette butts," she interrupts. She looks at me with a giant smile. "It seemed like there was smoke around his head so maybe he was smoking. We should look for cigarette butts. Maybe there'll be a trail of them."

The excitement in her voice is infectious.

"That's good. We could have those sent to a lab and see if we can get fingerprints or DNA."

"Seriously? Why?"

Because there's a psycho on the loose, and my gut is screaming at me that the man you saw and the identical wrecked vehicle are no coincidence.

I can't say any of that though, so I shrug. "Habit. Sorry."

I grab her hand, and we walk farther toward the trees. I watch as her gaze swings left and then right, taking in everything on the ground as we go. In this mode, it's easy to see that she would have made a damn good cop. She was the best prison guard I'd ever met, and that includes all of the ones I came into contact within the course of my job as a DEA agent.

About five feet beyond the tree line, I notice something that has my hair standing on end. A pile of cigarette butts next to a patch of grass that's clearly trampled, as if someone was standing in the spot for a while, wearing down the ground beneath their feet.

"What is it?" Emma asks from beside me.

"I think I found where the man was standing."

I point to the ground, and Emma crouches down to look at the spot. I stoop down next to her and watch as her eyes narrow and fear enters her expression.

"This isn't where I saw him, but…"

When she doesn't continue, I flatten my hand on her back between her shoulder blades. "But what?"

"Well, based on this, it seems pretty obvious." She stands and turns to face the road. "Whoever I saw had been here for a while. Watching the road. Waiting."

I heave a sigh. "That's what I was thinking."

"What were they waiting for though?"

Her voice sounds far away, like she's mentally somewhere else. Clearly she hasn't put together the exact same thought as me. That whoever it was standing here, whoever it was that she saw, was watching for *her*.

"Who knows?"

I shrug, pretending like I'm just as confused as she is. She's already shook up after being a 'sitting duck' as she called it. Until my suspicions are confirmed, no need to scare her even more. And maybe my gut will be wrong.

You don't really believe that.

My senses start to tingle, and I suddenly don't feel like we're alone. I turn in circles to scan the area but see nothing, no one. I can't shake the feeling though, so I guide Emma back to the tree line where we can stand in the open.

I yank my cell phone out of my pocket and dial Slade's number.

"Who're you calling?" she asks while I listen to the ringing.

"Slade."

"Surely you don't think that he…"

"Hey, man. What's up?" Slade answers, causing me to miss the rest of Emma's statement.

"I think I've got a crime scene for you." I waste no time with pleasantries.

Emma's eyes widen at my words, and her mouth opens to speak, but she slams it closed and remains silent.

"How the hell do you have a crime scene when you don't even work for the DEA anymore?" Slade snaps. He sounds on edge, and it makes me wonder if he has information on Lee that he hasn't shared.

It's probably just the job. Quit borrowing trouble.

I give Slade a quick rundown of the scene and why I'm

here. He interjects with a few questions, but in the end, he agrees to come and check it out.

"I owe ya one, man."

"It's not me you should be worried about." He chuckles. "My wife, on the other hand, she's the one who'll hurt you if I'm home late tonight. It's date night."

"Then I suggest you get your ass moving so you aren't late," I joke.

"I'll be there in a few."

Slade disconnects the call, and just before I can shove my phone in my pocket, a thought occurs to me.

"You should probably call Sierra and let her know you're okay." I hand my phone to Emma. She takes it but doesn't make the call. "What's wrong?" I ask when she stands there staring at the device.

"I don't know her number. It's programmed into my phone so I've never had to—"

"It's in my contacts," I say, a hint of embarrassment in my tone.

There are questions in her eyes, but she doesn't ask them. Instead, she scrolls through my meager contact list and presses a finger on Sierra's name when she gets to it. I listen as she reassures her best friend that she's 'fine' and with me. They talk for a few minutes, and from what I gather, movie night is still on.

"Thanks." Emma hands the phone to me. "She's going to hang out at my place until we get home." Emma glances over her shoulder into the trees. "It should be soon, right?"

A shiver wracks her body, but I doubt it's from the temperature of the air.

"Not too long," I assure her. "As soon as Slade gets here, I'll make sure he doesn't need anything from us and then we can go."

"Okay."

It's not lost on me that she doesn't suggest leaving on her own. She's got guts, that's for sure, but she also has a lot of fear.

We stand in silence for what seems like forever, but it is probably only ten minutes or so. Slade arrives and we both watch as he pulls his car off the side of the road and steps out. We walk toward him, and I shake his hand when we meet him halfway between the road and the tree line.

"Thanks for coming."

"No problem." Slade looks in the direction of the wrecked vehicle, letting out a low whistle at the damage. "Is this what you wanted me to see? Looks like law enforcement already handled the scene."

"That's part of it." I point at Emma's parked car. "Notice anything?"

Slade swings his gaze back and forth between the two cars. "Coincidence?" he asks when he returns his attention back to me.

"Could be," I concede. "But if I learned anything during my time in the DEA, it's that coincidences happen a lot less than people like to think."

"Isn't that the truth?" Slade looks at Emma. "What do you think about it?"

"About what? The cars being the same?" When Slade nods, she shrugs. "I don't know."

"Sure ya do," he prods. "You at least have an opinion about it."

"Well, I…" The column of Emma's throat works as she swallows. "I'm not sure what I'm supposed to think. I don't like it."

"Slade, come look at this."

I turn around and head toward the trees, not bothering to see if he follows. Emma quick steps to walk beside me, which tells me how she really feels about all of this. When I locate the pile of cigarette butts, I crouch down and wait for Slade.

"That sure adds to the mystery," he says when he's standing next to me.

"My thoughts exactly."

Slade walks around the area, kicking at leaves as if to uncover any additional evidence. I do the same, widening our search by approximately a twenty-foot radius. Emma remains rooted in place and follows us with watchful eyes.

"Got something," Slade calls from somewhere behind me.

I whirl around and walk toward where he's crouched down. I see what he's pointing at, and my heart drops into my stomach.

"Is that what I think it is?"

"If you think it's a spent shell casing for a high-powered rifle, then yes," Slade responds as he's pulling his cell phone out of his pocket.

"It could be from a hunter," I suggest, knowing I'm grasping at straws.

"And Santa Claus is real." Slade looks at me like I'm an idiot. "We both know this is too damn close to a main road for it to be from a hunter. Not to mention that it's an awful spot for hunting."

"Fuck!" I roar.

Slade begins barking orders into his phone, and when he seems satisfied, he hangs up. "I've got a team on the way. Why don't you two get out of here, and I'll come by after we process the scene?"

"Are you sure? What about date night?" I ask, knowing that date night is forgotten and taking a back seat to whatever the hell we stumbled on.

"Brandie will understand."

Slade sighs and braces his hands on his thighs to lever

himself up. He walks in circles in the immediate vicinity of the shell casing and mutters a curse under his breath.

"What?" I demand.

"Two more casings," he says as he thrusts a hand through his hair.

"What the fuck?" I grit out between clenched teeth.

I glance over my shoulder to where Emma is standing and hate the worry I see flitting across her face. I know she's heard what Slade and I have said, but she's remained silent and stoic.

"Get her home," Slade says quietly and tips his head at Emma. "I don't know her, but from what you've told me, she's been through enough and something tells me she's not going to like what we find out."

"I won't lie to her." I narrow my eyes at Slade. "She has a right to know what's going on."

"Yes, *she* does." Both Slade and I snap our eyes to Emma and watch as she steps closer to us. When she's within touching distance, she glares at Slade. "You're right, you don't know me. So let me fill you in." The fire in her tone reminds me of the prison guard in her. "I've had a shitty experience, but I don't need to be coddled or have information sugar coated. I don't like being in the dark about things, so don't even try to put me there."

"Sorry," Slade responds, sounding contrite. "Look, the truth is, this could all be one giant coincidence, but I don't think it is."

"Okay." Emma draws the word out. "What else could it be?"

"How much do you know about Jeffrey Lee?" Slade asks.

Emma's eyes grow wide at the mention of the man who attacked her.

"What's he got to do with this?" She directs the question to me.

"Emma, calm d—"

"Don't you dare tell me to calm down," she shouts and jabs a finger at my chest. "What the fuck does Lee have to do with all of this?" She sweeps her arm around to indicate what we found in the trees and the wrecked car.

Slade and I exchange a look, and Emma slaps my arm.

"Don't do that," she growls, her fury rising. "Don't look at each other like you have to figure out how to keep your story straight. Answer the damn question!"

I take a deep breath and rest my hands on her shoulders to steady her before I speak. "Lee escaped after the riot and has never been found."

Emma's entire body stiffens at the news, and color leeches from her cheeks. When she sways, I bend to scoop her into my arms and hug her to my chest.

"I promise you, doll," I whisper into her hair. "I won't let him hurt you."

19

EMMA

"What the hell, Em? Why don't you have a charger that works?"

I glare at Sierra as she continues to chastise me in front of Jett. She's not saying anything I don't already know, but I could do without the added embarrassment.

"I have a charger," I snap and immediately wish I could call the words back when I see the hurt look on Sierra's face. Jett tightens his arm around my waist, somehow sensing my need for comfort. My body deflates as the anger leaves me. "I'm sorry, Si."

"No, I'm sorry." Sierra steps forward and reaches out for a hug.

I move away from Jett and toward my best friend. She wraps her arms around me tightly, and the simple act fills me with a sense of calm that's as scary as the demons I've been fighting for two years.

Jett clears his throat, and Sierra and I pull apart. I slowly turn around to face him and place my hands on my hips.

He fights the grin tugging his lips, and I can't help the one on my own face.

"We'll get a charger first thing in the morning." Jett divides his attention between Sierra and me. "For now, why don't we just enjoy the rest of the night?"

"What's this 'we' stuff?" Sierra asks with laughter in her tone.

"Look, I know this is normally your girls' night or whatever." Jett waves his hand dismissively. "But tonight you're going to have to make room for a little testosterone." He pins me with his stare. "I'm not leaving."

"Fine by me," Sierra says and I swivel my head just in time to see her shrug. "Unless you've got a problem with that?" she asks me.

"Uh, no." I shake my head. "No problem."

"Good." Jett claps his hands and rubs them together. "So, what's for dinner?"

"I brought stuff to make breakfast for dinner." Sierra turns to walk to the kitchen, talking over her shoulder as she does. "When you took off like you did, I put everything away, but it won't take long to whip up some eggs, bacon, and French toast."

"Is there anything I can do to help?" Jett calls to Sierra.

"Nope. It's my night to cook and Em's night to pick the movies." Sierra leans against the doorframe between the kitchen and living room. "Maybe you could help her to pick the flick? She tends to pick sappy shit, and I'm in the mood for something a little... more." She returns to the task of fixing dinner.

Left alone with Jett, my mind races and my heart beats frantically. I hoped that being around him more would make me feel more comfortable, but exactly the opposite has happened. I feel incredibly *uncomfortable* in the most unexpected way.

Ignoring his stare, I walk to the couch, picking up the remote control before I sit down. I press buttons until

Netflix is pulled up and begin scrolling through the movies. The cushion dips when Jett sits next to me, and my heart skips a beat.

"What're we watching?"

I glance at him out of the corner of my eye and sigh. "I don't know." My shoulders sag. "I guess Sierra isn't up for our usual."

"Sappy shit?" Jett teases.

"I guess you could call it that."

Jett plucks the remote from my hand, and when I try to grab it back, he raises it above his head out of my reach. This happens several times before Jett uses his free hand to pull me into his chest and hold me there. For a split second, my muscles tense, and Jett must sense it because he loosens his hold.

"I'm not going to hurt you," he whispers in my ear, causing a shiver to race down my spine.

"I know that," I say on an exhale.

"I'm not so sure about that, but I think you're getting there."

I lock eyes with him, and the intensity I see matches my own. It's on the tip of my tongue to argue that I do trust him, but I don't say the words. Instead, I let my actions do my talking for me.

Leaning forward, I see Jett's eyes widen the moment right before my lips touch his. When the kiss doesn't deepen, I start to lean back, only to have Jett move his hand from my waist to the back of my head. The pressure he uses to keep me in place is intoxicating, and I cease trying to move away.

Jett's tongue darts out, and he licks the seam of my lips and urges them open. I grant him access, and heat rushes through me until I feel like my body is on fire. We kiss like we're meant for each other, and I find the thought comforting and completely foreign.

JETT'S GUARD

Lost in bliss, it takes longer than I care to admit to hear someone clearing their throat. When it does register, I toss a look over my shoulder and see Sierra standing in the doorway with a giant grin on her face.

"What?" I snap, embarrassed to have been caught.

"Nothing." Sierra hitches her thumb toward the kitchen. "Dinner's ready."

Without waiting for a response, she returns to the kitchen, once again, leaving me alone with Jett. When I return my attention to him, his eyes are dark and stormy.

"We, uh, we should eat," I stammer. I swallow past the lump in my throat and avert my gaze.

Jett says nothing, but he rises from the couch and sticks a hand out to help me up. I rest my palm against his, and strong fingers wrap around mine. When we're both standing, he doesn't release my hand as he guides me toward the kitchen.

Sierra is filling her plate to the brim with delicious smelling food, and my stomach growls at the smells wafting from the stove. Jett looks at me with one arched brow and smiles. I brush past him to fill my own plate, and he follows suit.

Once we're all done in the kitchen, we return to the living room. Sierra sits on the overstuffed chair while Jett sits next to me.

"You pick a movie?" Sierra asks when she glances at the television.

When I don't respond, Jett fills the silence. "I wasn't sure what you'd like, so why don't you pick?"

"I can't pick," Sierra retorts as she shakes her head. "It's Emma's turn."

"I don't mind, Si. We can watch whatever you want."

That's not how Sierra and I do things. When it's your turn to pick the movie, you pick the movie. And no matter what you pick, the other can't complain. It's what we've done for years, and I'm not sure how I feel about switching things up. But I can't think straight with Jett so close, so I don't bother trying to examine my feelings about a damn movie.

"If you're sure," Sierra mumbles.

She picks up the remote and searches through Netflix, finally settling on an action movie that I've never heard of before. Sierra hits play and we all dig into our food as the opening credits roll.

When Jett finishes eating, he glances at my empty plate in my hands. He stands and takes our plates to the kitchen, and when he returns, he sits closer to me than before, his knee bumping mine. The zing that ricochets through me at the contact is becoming more and more familiar the more time I spend with Jett. And I love it.

Forty-five minutes into the movie, Jett stretches his arm around my shoulders and pulls me into his side. I can't hold in the sigh that escapes. I glance at Sierra out of the corner of my eye to see if she notices, but her eyelids are drooping and I know she's close to sleep. I remain in Jett's embrace for the remainder of the movie, and when the ending credits roll, I recognize the pang of sadness that hits me. I'm not ready to leave the warmth of his body.

Jett removes his arm and sits up on the couch, bracing his forearms on his knees. With his fingers interlaced, he looks incredibly serious and just a little bit distraught.

"What's wrong?" I ask, uncertainty in my tone.

"What?" He whips his head in my direction. "Nothing's wrong."

"Then why do you look like you just lost your best friend?"

"Sorry, just thinking."

"About?" I ask when he doesn't offer any further information.

Jett stands up and shoves his hands in his pockets. He tilts his head toward Sierra and asks, "Is she staying?"

His question confuses me, and I stand to face him. "Yeah, she always stays. Why?"

He shoves a hand through his hair, causing it to stand on end. "Because I'm staying. And I'm not so sure she's going to be able to sleep through the noise."

"What noise?"

Jett reaches out and runs the tip of his finger down my check, over my collarbone and in between my breasts. A moan escapes at the sensations he's evoking, and my head falls back. His lips press to the pulse-point at my throat, licking where it thumps for him.

"That noise," he growls in my ear when my moans turn into pleading cries.

20

JETT

Hearing Emma beg for me is a sound I'll never tire of and one that causes my cock to swell almost painfully behind the zipper of my jeans. I clasp my hands under her ass and lift her up, loving the way her legs go around my waist instinctually.

"You're in control," I whisper.

She buries her face in my shoulder and nods.

"Em, I need to know you understand." I make my way up the stairs, toward her bedroom. "If you want me to stop, just say so." I follow up my statement with a nibble on her ear and feel her lips part on my neck.

"I… yes, I understand," she says with a sigh.

I continue my assault on her neck and blindly walk into her room. The layout of it is burned into my memory from the night I came running to the rescue, and when I reach the bed I loosen my hold to let Emma fall to the mattress. She tightens her grip around my neck, taking me with her.

I brace myself on outstretched arms and gaze down at her. Emma's expressions betray a bit of the uncertainty she's feeling, and I consider getting up and going home. Then I remember the car accident from earlier and the note that was left at her door and dismiss any thought of leaving her.

I lean down and press my lips against hers, tease and tempt her with sweeps of my tongue. Within seconds, her body relaxes and the moans from earlier return. Emma wraps her arms around my back and pulls me down so my body is flush with hers.

Emma rocks her hips, pressing her pelvis into mine, and my dick jumps. Her hands smooth down my spine until her palms are flat against my ass, begging me to fuck her. I pull my mouth from hers and search her eyes.

"Are you sure?"

I give her one last time to back out. Not that I won't stop later if that's what she wants, but I'm praying it isn't.

Emma nods her head, and that's all the invitation I need. I rise to my feet, yank my shirt over my head and toss it to the floor. Her eyes widen when my chest is bare, but her mouth tilts into a grin. I watch as her stare roams over my torso and recognize the moment she spots the scar from the night of the riot.

"It's not as bad as it looks," I assure her.

Her eyes glaze over, and I wonder if she heard me. She no longer seems to be present in the moment, but rather trapped in the memories in her head. I cup her cheek and rub her skin with the pad of my thumb.

"Emma, look at me." When she doesn't, I repeat myself with more authority. "Emma, I need you to look at me, doll."

She blinks several times and refocuses her stare on my face. Her lashes are spiked with tears, but she doesn't let them fall. I reach for her hand and bring it to the puckered flesh, flattening her palm against the reminder of both of our demons.

"Did it hurt?" Her voice is barely above a whisper, and I have to strain to hear her.

"Not so much." That's a lie, but it's one I'm comfortable telling if it'll make her feel better. "Adrenaline masked the pain."

Emma gives a curt nod and, on her own, traces the line of the scar. She leans in and brushes her lips against it and the contact, along with her face so close to my dick, heats my blood. When she lingers, I have to take a step back or I'll blow like some inexperienced teenager.

Hurt flashes across her face, but she quickly masks it. After a few deep breaths and the mental recitation of the Pledge of Allegiance, I close the distance between us, reasonably sure that I won't embarrass myself.

"I want you, Jett." Crimson stains her cheeks. "So damn bad, but…"

I wait for her to finish her sentence, knowing that she will when she's ready. I could finish it for her, but what purpose would that serve, other than to take control of the situation? No, she's in charge, no matter how much my body protests and demands otherwise.

"I'm scared," she finally manages.

"I know." I tug her up to stand in front of me, pulling her body flush with mine. "But you know I won't hurt you. I could never hurt you."

"It's not that."

"Then what is it? What are you afraid of?"

"What if I'm broken… that way? What if I have flashbacks in the middle of it? What if I—"

"What if you aren't?" I shut down her line of thinking. "What if it's exactly as it should be? I don't think it's a matter of what goes wrong but rather a matter of what all can go perfectly right." Emma inhales deeply, and when she exhales, her breath skitters across my flesh. "Besides, if I'm doing my job, there's not going to be any room in your head for anything but the moment and me."

"Okay."

"Okay?"

Emma nods. "Okay."

That's all the permission I need. I fuse my lips to hers and lift her up, reveling in the way she locks her ankles at the small of my back. She's still clothed, but I'll rectify that soon enough.

With Emma in my arms, I turn around and sit on the bed, urging her to straddle me. She does without breaking the kiss. My cock twitches at the friction and the thought of having her pussy so close. She grinds against me as if she never had any reservations and the previous few minutes never happened.

"Naked," I say into her mouth. "I need you naked."

She yanks her shirt over her head, and when she reaches behind her to unhook her blue lace bra, I stop her.

"Let me?"

I deftly flick the clasps open and slowly slide the straps over her shoulders and down her arms. When she's free of it, I toss it to the floor where it joins our shirts. I cup her tits in my hands and pinch her nipples, tweaking and teasing her.

Emma's head falls back, exposing the column of her throat. I lean in and lick near her pulse point and then trace a path down to a nipple and draw it in between my lips. I swirl my tongue around the puckered peak, and she bucks wildly.

In a lightning fast move, I twist with her in my arms and lay her out on the bed beneath me. I continue my assault on her nipple as I reach between our bodies and unbutton her jeans. Emma reaches between us at the same time and shoves her small hand into my boxer briefs and fists my dick. She runs her thumb over the slit, smearing pre-cum around the sensitive tip.

I yank her hand away, not ready for this to end as quickly as it will if she continues. I slide down her torso, down her legs, and pull her pants and panties off in one swift move. When Emma's naked, I take a moment to devour the sight of her, the way her skin flushes under my scrutiny and her knees shake almost imperceptibly.

"Exquisite," I murmur as I memorize every detail. The freckle on her right hipbone, the birthmark on her left thigh, the way her waist dips in and her hips flare. "Absolute fucking perfection."

I kneel next to the bed and grip her thighs to tug her toward me. Her aroused scent fills my nostrils when I bury my face between her legs. I hum against her clit, and she quivers and moans. Tentatively, I flick the sensitive ball of nerves with the tip of my tongue and grip Emma's hips to hold her in place.

"More... I need more," she groans as her head thrashes from side to side.

Unable to deny this woman anything, I slide one finger into her pussy and her walls spasm. I work my finger in and out of her while I increase the speed and pressure of my mouth on her clit. I add a finger and twist my wrist so my hand is palm up and then crook both digits.

Emma's hips shoot off the bed, and I brace my forearm across her stomach to hold her down. I slow my movements until I feel her body start to relax and I'm confident she's no longer on that ragged edge of release.

I shift from between her legs to crawl up her body and fist my cock as I do. I watch Emma's eyes, pay attention to her every reaction. I line up with her pussy and slowly enter her wet heat. When she practically purrs, it takes every ounce of restraint I possess to not impale her in one forceful thrust.

I rock my hips as I glide in and out, going deeper every time. I'm balls deep in heaven, and the pleasure only intensifies. Emma matches me, thrust for thrust. Her hands are on my ass, her nails digging into my skin, but I feel no pain.

We fuck in a frenzy of slapping flesh and guttural moans. Emma's tongue darts out, and I lean in to capture it. Our mouths mimic the rhythm of our bodies, and I swallow every sound she makes as if it's feeding my soul.

"Ah, oh fuck… I, I'm gonna… Holy shit…" Emma continues to murmur, and her body begins to quake.

I thrust with the ferocity of a man possessed and slide my hand down to rub her clit with my thumb. With the added stimulation, her hips buck.

"That's it, doll," I growl in her ear. "Come for me."

As soon as the words leave my mouth, her pussy clenches and unclenches in quick succession as her orgasm crashes over her like a tidal wave. Her ecstasy drives me over the edge with her, and I shout out my release.

When the intensity begins to ease, I slow my strokes, and when her arms and legs go lax, I roll to her left, taking her with me and pulling her into my chest. Emma throws a leg over my thigh and sighs.

I want to say something, anything, but I have no words to adequately describe what's going through my head.

"That was…" Emma shakes her head which leads me to believe she can't find the words either.

Fuck it. One of us has to say it.

"Perfect."

21

EMMA

A light touch on my shoulder pulls me from sleep in a rush. I shoot up into a sitting position and take in my surroundings. My room is still dark which tells me that it's not morning. Slowly my vision adjusts, and I'm able to make out Sierra standing next to my bed.

Jett stirs behind me, and his nudity caresses my body as he sits up. My pussy clenches at the contact. I force my thoughts and attention to Sierra, who looks rumpled from sleep. Her eyes are wide and glued to the gloriously naked man behind me.

"I don't think you're going to find the reason you came in here on my body," Jett says to Sierra with a chuckle in his voice.

"Sorry." Sierra spits the words out as she lowers her gaze. "But seriously, Em, he's fucking sex on a stick."

"And he's right here," Jett reminds her.

"Sorry, again."

"Did you need something?" I ask her. A glance at my phone tells me it's four in the morning, and while I love

Sierra to death, I want her to leave so I can do more wicked things with the man in my bed.

"Oh, right." She shakes her head as if to rid herself of the last few minutes. "There's someone at your door."

"Who?" Jett snaps, throwing off the covers and jumping out of bed to pick up his discarded clothes from the floor. As he's tugging his jeans up his legs, he seems hyper-focused and alert.

"Says his name is Len," Sierra responds with confusion wrinkling her forehead. "Hey, Em, isn't that the doctor from the prison?"

"What the fuck is he doing here?" Jett demands and glances at his own phone when he pulls it from his pocket. "And at this hour?"

I scramble out of bed, not bothering to cover myself while I dig through my dresser for a pair of sweats and a t-shirt. My mind races with the possibilities of what brings Len to my door, and none of them are good.

Ignoring both Jett and Sierra's questioning looks, I traipse downstairs and see Len standing by the front door. *Sierra just left him here? Alone?*

When Len spots me, he rushes forward and throws his arms around me and pulls me toward him. I cringe at the contact and manage to extricate myself from his hold. In the seconds that it takes for this to transpire, Jett is beside me, and if I'm not mistaken, he's growling at Len.

"Why the hell is he here?" Len sneers while staring daggers at Jett.

"I could ask you the same thing," Jett grits out. He narrows his eyes at Len and tosses his arm casually over my shoulders, tucking me into his side.

Len bristles and pure rage enters his eyes, taking them from a dull brown to a sparking gold fire. He darts his gaze back and forth between me and Jett, swallowing several times and visibly trying to maintain his composure. Finally, he settles his attention on me, and his body seems to deflate.

"I was worried about you, Emma," Len says softly, but the concern he's trying to portray falls short. "I heard about the accident, and I had to see for myself that you were okay."

Stunned by his quick shift in mood, his words don't immediately register, but the tightening of Jett's hold on me does. I glance up at him, narrowing my eyes, and he releases me.

"What the fuck do you know about the accident?" Jett advances toward Len, closing the five-foot distance, and Len backs up until he runs into the door.

Len bristles and squares his shoulders. "You can't talk to me like that." He shifts his attention to me. "Are you going to let him talk to me like that, Emma?"

"We're not in the fucking cage, *Doc*." Jett's tone is laced with steel. "And Emma doesn't *let* me do anything. I'm a grown ass man." He leans in close, only inches from Len's face. "Now, I'll ask you again. What the fuck do you know about the accident?"

"Jett?" I step up to his back, flattening my palm between his shoulder blades. He doesn't so much as acknowledge me. "Jett!"

I watch as his shoulders rise and fall a few times before he looks over his shoulder at me and his face softens.

"Yeah, doll?"

"I'm really thirsty. Would you get me some water?"

He arches a brow at me. "Seriously?"

"Please?" I let my mouth tip into a smile. "I'll be fine. I promise."

My heart rate says otherwise, and the only thing I know to do is separate the two of them because seeing them act like this, all big and bad, sends my mind to places it doesn't want to go. The thing about not being honest though, is that people that know you, *really* know you, can see right through the lie. And apparently Jett really knows me because he smirks as if to say 'We'll talk about this later' and turns back around to face Len.

"I'm watching you," he threatens and then spins around to head to the kitchen.

When I hear him banging around in the cupboards, I refocus on Len.

"I'm afraid you were misinformed." I try to keep my voice professional even though we are no longer coworkers. He needs to know that we won't ever be anything more than that to me: an old coworker from a time in my life that I'd rather forget. Then a thought occurs to me. "Where *did* you hear about the accident?"

For a split second, Len looks like a kid who got caught with his hand in the cookie jar. But the look is gone faster than it appeared, and I convince myself that I'm seeing things, making more of the situation than there is.

"It was on the news," he replies smoothly. "I worked a later shift, and I always record the news. When I got home, I watched it and then came straight here. I was so worried."

"Yeah, so you already said," I mumble under my breath.

"What?"

"Nothing." I cross my arms over my chest, suddenly very aware that I didn't put a bra on and feeling more exposed than I should. "As you can see, I'm fine."

"Yes, but—"

"It wasn't me in the accident, Len," I grate out. Alarm bells are going off in my head but I shove them aside. I managed to put the whole evening out of my head and focus on my time with Jett, and Len is making that virtually impossible now. "It was just a car that looked like mine."

Len looks confused, but again, he masks it quickly. "Oh."

Is that disappointment in his voice?

I feel Jett's body heat at my back before I hear him. I also catch a glimpse of Sierra as she stands at the bottom of the staircase, arms crossed over her chest.

"What news station did you say you heard this on?" Jett asks and his tone is calm but controlled. He reaches around me to give me the glass of water before settling his hands at my hips in a gesture meant to stake his claim.

"Uh, I think..." Len pauses and clears his throat. "Channel nine."

"Is that an answer or a question?" Jett demands.

"It was channel nine," Len snaps, letting some of his anger slip out. "What does that matter?"

"Well, we were at the scene, and I don't recall any news crews being there so I find it curious that you show up in the middle of the night and claim to have seen it on TV."

"Are you accusing me of lying?" Len's face hardens.

"Nope," Jett says easily. "Wouldn't dream of it, *Doc*. Just trying to sort out the facts."

"Look, Len," I interrupt, tired of dragging this out and knowing that I'm the only one that can put a stop to it. "Thanks for checking on me, but it wasn't necessary. I'm fine as you can see. Now, I think it's time for you to go."

I nod toward the door behind him. He stares at me like I've lost my mind. Granted, he doesn't know that Jett isn't actually a felon, but even if he was, that's my business and my choice to make. It definitely doesn't concern Len, no matter how much he claims to care.

When Len makes no move to leave, Jett starts to go around me, and the sound coming from his throat is menacing. Once again, he's in Len's face, but this time Len puffs his chest out and doesn't back down.

"You heard her," Jett snarls. "It's time for you to go."

"I heard her," Len snaps. "And I'm leaving." Len forces his

eyes to meet mine. "I hope you know what you're doing, Emma. I'd hate for something to happen to you because of the company you keep."

With those parting words, he turns on his heel and storms out the door, slamming it closed behind him. I release a breath I didn't know I was holding, and my shoulders deflate. The thud of his feet on the front porch steps reaches me, and I can't help but wonder where this *tougher* Len was the night of the riot.

"Where are you going?" I ask Jett when he pulls the door open and steps out onto the porch.

"Just making sure the prick leaves."

"Holy shit," Sierra says as she rushes forward to stand next to me, both of us staring out the door after Jett. "That was... I don't know what that was."

"It was nothing. Just Len being Len."

Sierra shakes her head. "I don't think so, Em. There's a screw loose with that one."

Hearing her utter the words that mirror my own thoughts so closely is unnerving. I don't want to admit it, but that entire scene with Len has me shaken and more than a little concerned. When Jett returns, I quickly close the door behind him and flip the lock. Somehow, that doesn't make me feel as safe as it would have even an hour ago.

"He left?" I ask Jett, even though I know he wouldn't have returned if he hadn't.

"Yeah, he did." Jett looks to Sierra. "Where did you put the bags I had when I showed up yesterday?"

"Oh, um, I put them in the closet." She hitches her thumb over her shoulder to indicate the coat closet.

Jett retrieves them and stalks toward the kitchen, where he empties the bags and scatters the contents on the counter. Sierra and I share a look, and she shrugs as if to say 'no idea'.

"What is all this?" I ask, stepping up next to Jett and

picking up what looks to be a very expensive piece of equipment.

"Just some stuff I picked up yesterday to make your house a little safer."

"Jett, this is more than 'just some stuff'. My kitchen is starting to look like a war room."

Jett snorts out a laugh. "Not quite. But there is enough here to ensure that you've got the best in home security and defense."

"Why would she need all of this?" Sierra asks and I wince, remembering that I haven't yet told her about the note.

Jett looks at me with raised eyebrows. "You didn't tell her?"

"Tell me what?" Sierra demands. She crosses her arms over her chest and taps her foot in a move that's usually reserved for when she's getting really pissed. "What's going on?"

I take a deep breath and then launch into details about the note that I thought Jett had left for me. The entire time I'm talking, Sierra's expression shifts from angry to worried. I fill her in on the man I saw at the scene of the accident and how Jett's friend, Slade, is working on trying to sort through that. By the time I'm done, I'm drained and all I want to do is go back to bed.

Jett must sense that because he says, "Why don't the two of you go upstairs and crawl into bed. You can talk up there if you want or you can sleep." He tips his head toward his purchases. "I'm going to work on getting all of this installed."

"Do you really think this is necessary?" I ask already knowing the answer.

Jett takes a step toward me and rests his hands on my shoulders, giving them a squeeze. "Do you trust me, doll?"

In this moment, staring in his eyes and seeing the

emotion there, I know for sure that I do trust him. On some level, I think I already knew that, but I feel like I can admit it now without any residual fear lingering.

"With my life."

22

JETT

"There's nothing, man."

I rake my fingers through my hair. As soon as I was sure that Emma and Sierra were upstairs behind a closed door, I called Slade. Not only did I want an update from the accident scene, but good ol' Len stopping by isn't sitting right with me.

"Goddammit!"

"I've checked him out as thoroughly as I can. Len Harden has a few parking tickets and some shitty life experiences, but no criminal record, nothing that ties him to Lee."

"I'm telling you, Slade, we're missing something. We have to be."

"Listen, Jett. Maybe you're wrong about this."

"I'm not fucking wrong," I snap. I pace the length of Emma's living room, grateful for the area rugs and the way they muffle my steps. Recognizing that Slade isn't who I need to take my frustration out on, I take a deep breath and blow it out. "Sorry. It's not your fault. I just want to—"

"Protect your girl," he interrupts quietly.

"She's not…" I don't finish my sentence because it would

be a lie. I don't know when it happened, whether it was while I was undercover or when I was taking her grocery shopping or as recently as when we slept together, but he's right. She's mine, in every way that matters. "Okay, yeah. She's mine and I won't lose her. Not to some psycho."

"Does she know you've staked your claim?"

"Shit, I don't know. I think so. I haven't hidden how I feel about her."

"But you haven't made it completely clear, either, have you?"

Slade's questions are shifting my focus, and while thoughts of Emma are the best distraction, the *only* distraction, I need to remember why I called him.

"So we have nothing to confirm a connection between Lee and Len. What about the accident scene? Were you able to find anything there after we left?"

"Not too much. We found more cigarette butts and bagged them for testing. I called in a local tracker, and he was able to find and follow footprints back through the woods to a clearing next to a dirt road. It was clear that a car was parked there. No idea if it's our guy, but we took impressions and we'll see what we get from that."

"In other words, nothing."

"No, not nothing. Just nothing conclusive at the moment. I put a rush on all the testing so we should have that back in a few days. In the meantime, keep doing what you're doing and make sure that Emma remains vigilant."

"Oh, no worries on that front. I'm getting ready to install a shitton of security equipment at her house that I got just before everything went down last night."

Silence ensues and I think back over our conversation, trying to determine if I have any other questions. One comes to mind.

"Hey, man," I begin, knowing what I'm going to ask puts

Slade at risk. "Any chance you can send me all the information you dug up on Len and all the reports that were looked at to see if there was a tie to Lee? I know it's—"

"Absolutely." He doesn't even hesitate. "We all have different ways of looking at things. Maybe you'll catch something that we didn't. If nothing else, your gut is telling you something for a reason and maybe something will jump out at you."

"Thanks, man. I know you can get in trouble for that, but I appreciate it."

"Don't mention it. Besides, you'd do the same for me."

He's right. I would. Slade and I may not have been anything beyond work acquaintances, but all of the bullshit that he, Jackson, and I have dealt with since taking down two major players in the criminal underworld, we've gotten close. I'd take a bullet for him, without question, and he would do the same.

"I'll get it all scanned and email it over to you. It may take an hour or so. There's a lot there."

"No problem. I'm going to get shit on my end installed and that's going to take a few hours."

"Sounds good. Listen, call me if you find anything, okay?"

"Slade, if I find something, if I can prove my suspicions, you aren't going to want to know. Plausible deniability and all that."

"Jett, don't do anything stupid," he warns.

"And if we were dealing with Brandie?" I taunt.

Slade swears viciously under his breath. "Fine. Just don't do anything I wouldn't do."

"Wouldn't dream of it."

I end the call before Slade can change his mind. I shove my phone in my pocket and get to work.

After getting everything set up, I ran to my house to grab my laptop and now I'm sitting on Emma's couch with Freedom sound asleep at my feet. All of the installed cameras are functioning properly, and I've got a clear view of all sides of her house. I have additional cameras that I'll put up at my place, which will give me an even broader view of what's going on.

Scrolling through the documents that Slade emailed, I click on the link for one labeled 'Work Emails' and wait for it to load. It takes several minutes as it's a large file, but when it's done, every email sent and received by Len Harden at his prison employee email address pops up on my screen.

There are numerous emails that have nothing even remotely incriminating. Memo's from the prison warden, inappropriate jokes from a few of the guards, and even some promotional emails that Len must have signed up to receive. Just when I think this file is going to be a dead end, I stumble on a few that Len sent, requesting to have his shifts changed.

I open up another tab in my internet browser and create a new spreadsheet in Google Drive. I go through each email and enter the dates that he made the requests and the shifts he was requesting to work. What immediately strikes me is that the most recent request was submitted a week ago, and it was in relation to his shift last night.

After I go through all of those, I come across another set of emails that have subject lines filled with numbers only. I skim through each one to see if anything jumps out at me, and when nothing does, I go back through them very slowly, making a point to read every word.

In the middle of reading the sixth email I start to notice certain phrases that are used frequently. Phrases like 'communication is key', 'inner circle' and 'training facilitator'. On the surface, these phrases aren't anything alarming, but the rate at which they appear, along with the other contents in the emails, causes a knot of dread to form in the pit of my stomach.

I create another spreadsheet where I enter the dates of the emails, the phrases that appear in each of them, the numbers in the subject lines and the sender and/or receiver's email address.

"What are you doing?"

Emma's voice startles me, and I cringe at the fact that I didn't hear her coming down the steps. Some protector I am. I shift on the couch so I can look at her, and when I take in her rumpled hair and sleepy eyes, I smile.

"How'd you sleep?" I ask, rather than answer her question.

"Not as good as I would have if you were sharing my bed instead of Sierra." She walks around the couch and sits down next to me. "She's a bed hog. And she snores."

I chuckle at the way her nose crinkles when she speaks. "Good to know."

"You didn't answer my question," she says and tilts her head toward my laptop screen.

I close the lid of the computer and set it on the coffee table. "Nothing. Just a little research."

"Why'd you close it?" Her eyes narrow with suspicion. "I don't do secrets, Jett. Or lies."

"I'm not lying," I say on an exhale.

"But you are keeping something from me." Her words are a statement of the facts as she sees them.

I rise to my feet and start toward the kitchen. "Are you hungry?" I ask over my shoulder.

"Don't you dare walk away from me." Her voice rises, and it's filled with anger so I turn back around to face her. If looks could kill, I'd be on my way to six feet under.

"I'll fill you in on what I was looking at. I promise." I close the distance between us and grab her hand to guide her to the kitchen. "But first, food."

"You've got two minutes to pour us both a bowl of cereal and then you're gonna start talking."

"Yes, ma'am."

It takes me one minute and forty-five seconds—yes, I counted—to complete my task, and when we're both seated at the table, I start eating.

"Time's up."

"I know," I say around a mouth full of Cinnamon Toast Crunch. After swallowing, I launch into my explanation. "I was going over information that Slade sent me."

"Information about what?"

"Len," I say, not trying to sugarcoat it. She wants answers and the truth and she'll get it. "I asked him to look into Len after you received that note. Slade and his team weren't able to learn anything helpful from it, so he sent it to me to see if I could make sense of what was there."

"And?" Emma tilts her head. "Did you find anything?"

"I'm not sure," I answer honestly. "There are a set of emails that set off warning bells in my head."

"Is there something specific that you're looking for? Anything I can do to help?

"Actually, yes." I nod as I warm up to the idea. "You can help. You worked with him. Between you and me, you know him better. Maybe you could take a look at what Slade sent over and see if anything seems off to you."

"I can do that." Emma's anger seems to fade as quickly as it came. "You didn't answer my other question."

"What other question?"

"What, specifically, are you looking for?"

Well, shit. You avoided this question for a reason, but it doesn't matter now.

"Anything that doesn't seem right, and," I pause and take a deep breath. "Anything that could tie Len to Lee."

"Wait." Her brow furrows. "Lee, as in the guy you went undercover for?"

"The one and only."

Emma gives a curt nod. "Okay. Let's get to work."

With that, she carries her unfinished cereal to the sink and dumps it before going to the living room and grabbing my laptop and getting comfortable on the couch.

"You coming?" she hollers from the other room.

Shocked by her quick acceptance, I shovel the rest of my cereal into my mouth and put my empty bowl with her discarded one. When I join Emma on the couch, I'm surprised to see she got past the password and is already digging into the information.

When I give her a questioning look, she shrugs. "'Freedom' wasn't exactly hard to figure out. You should change that password."

Shaking my head at her, I reach for the laptop and pull up the spreadsheets and explain what I started to track. She catches on quickly, and before long, she's got her own laptop out and we're both sorting through documents and adding to the spreadsheets.

"Oh my God," she mumbles about two hours later. "Jett, look at this. I think I've figured something out."

I set my own computer aside and scoot closer to her so I can see what she has. I scan the screen, and my heart skips a beat when it hits me what she uncovered.

"Please tell me I'm wrong," Emma pleads. "That this is all a mistake."

23

EMMA

*I*t's been a week since I discovered Len's secret. One week since Jett made me feel alive again, only to have it all torn away by cryptic emails and sadistic men. Seven fucking days of wanting to crawl out of my skin but being trapped.

"I still don't know how I missed this."

Jett's anger at our revelation hasn't waned in two days. If anything, it's intensified to the point that I worry he might never rid himself of it. That and the guilt. I've lost count of the number of times he's apologized, the number of times I've told him 'It's fine'.

"You've gotta stop beating yourself up about this," Slade says from his spot at Jett's kitchen table.

"I've told him that." I glance at Jett out of the corner of my eye. "Several times."

"How are you so calm about this?" Jett demands. "That night destroyed your life. And there's still a huge threat out there."

"Calm?" I rise from my chair and start to pace, my voice getting higher the more I talk. "Calm? I'm not calm. I'm holding on by a thread. A very thin, frayed thread. But it's not your fault!" I shout as I whirl on him.

"You're wrong, Em." Jett gets to his feet and stomps toward me, gripping my shoulders when he's near. "I put you in this position. If I'd—"

"Both of you," Slade cuts in, and his fist connects with the table. "Stop!" Jett and I simultaneously face Slade. "Jett, it's not your fault that Emma became a target. Lee's good at what he does. If he wasn't, he'd be back behind bars or dead. Whether or not you take him down doesn't change the fact that you love her and would do anything to keep her safe. Remember that." He takes a deep breath and focuses on me. "Emma, Jett's going to blame himself no matter what you or I say. It's what men like us do. All you can do is show him that you love him no matter what. And let him protect you, let him do whatever it is he feels he needs to do."

"I don't… he doesn't…"

"We don't…"

Jett and I mutter at the same time, and all Slade does is stand there and laugh at us, shaking his head.

"Yeah, you do love each other. You're both just too scared to admit it."

My face warms, and I know it's turning an embarrassing shade of crimson. I scan the room and look everywhere but at Jett. Love him? I don't know about that. I like him… a lot. I want to see where things go between us once the threat is gone. But love? No. Nope. Not possi—

Jett clears his throat, causing me to jump at the intrusion into my thoughts. "Can we just focus? Please?"

"Sure. I can," Slade says. "Can you?"

"Goddammit!" Jett snaps. "Yes, I can fucking focus."

"Fine." Slade sits back down and spreads out the printed emails and the spreadsheet that was instrumental in helping to sort everything out. "Let's review what we know."

Both Jett and I sit down across from Slade, and our elbows bump. I focus on the documents, but when Jett's hand rests on my thigh under the table, I can't help the sigh that escapes.

"We know that the riot was orchestrated by Jeffrey Lee," Jett begins. He squeezes my knee as he continues as if to remind me that he's here. "We know that Len Harden knew that there was going to be a riot, but he wasn't aware of when it would happen."

"Lee's plan all along was to incapacitate me." I pick up where Jett leaves off. "He figured if I was in the infirmary, I was an easy target. What he didn't count on was Jett actually stepping in to help me."

"Right," Slade confirms. "It wasn't difficult to get Len on board because Lee promised him that he could have you as payment for his help." Slade nods in my direction. "He knew you'd never agree to go out with him and figured the only way he'd get you was to *buy* you."

"What I don't get is why me." It's a question I've asked myself a million times in the last two years, but the last seven days has given it all new meaning.

"Have you looked in a mirror lately?" Slade retorts, and when Jett lets out a low growl, Slade holds up his hands in mock surrender. "Sorry, man, but come on. She's hot. Not to mention smart as hell and sweet as can be."

"You've got your own woman. Leave mine alone."

My head snaps in Jett's direction, and I stare at him with wide eyes. "Yours?"

I watch in fascination as Jett's jaw tenses and he grinds his teeth. His eyes darken, and his stare becomes intense.

"You're my responsibility, so yeah."

My heart shatters at his words. I don't want to be his responsibility. I don't want to be anyone's responsibility. I want to be someone's *one*.

"Right, of course," I mumble and refocus on the documents on the table. I take a deep breath, and my shoulders drop when I exhale. "What do we do now? How do we catch them?"

"I have an idea," Slade says. "But you're not gonna like it."

∾

"Do you want me to cancel movie night?"

Jett is pacing his living room, Freedom at his heels. Sierra is expected at my house in an hour, but since Slade unveiled his grand plan, Jett's been on edge. I really want to spend time with my best friend, alone, and am hoping Jett gets that.

"I want you to, yes." He comes to a stop in front of me and cups my cheek. "But I won't ask you to do that."

When his lips touch mine, my knees wobble, and I twist my hands in his shirt to hold on. The kiss is slow, passionate and full of so much emotion that I feel as if I'll burst with it. Jett nips at my bottom lip, and my mouth curves against his.

"What was that for?" I ask when the connection is broken.

"Just because." Jett places one last peck on my cheek before dropping his arms to his sides and taking a few deep breaths. "Go, have fun with Sierra. I'll keep an eye on things from here."

As much as I was just thinking I need time alone with her, now I find it hard to walk away from him. I break eye contact and bend to run my fingers through Freedom's fur, putting off leaving. When I stop, Freedom nudges my hand for more. I oblige her for a few more minutes but eventually realize that I have to leave or Sierra will worry when I'm not home.

"C'mon, doll." Jett throws his arms around my shoulder. "I'll walk you over."

We reach my house, and Jett does a sweep of every room

to make sure that no evil lurks. When he pronounces it safe, he reminds me to call him if I need anything and promises to come over in the morning.

Left alone with nothing but the sound of the radio to drown out the silence, I flip through online menus on my phone to figure out what to get for dinner. It's Sierra's turn to pick the movie which means it's my turn to feed us.

My thoughts drift to another online menu, one only found on the dark web and that lists humans as appetizers, entrees and desserts. A menu that I'm now a 'featured dish' on, courtesy of the FBI. I cringe when I remember the picture that accompanies my description. It's photoshopped, but it doesn't make me feel any less vulnerable. I'm still amazed at how quickly Slade was able to pull everything together since leaving this morning, but—

A knock on the door startles me from my thoughts, and a glance at the time on my phone tells me I drifted into la-la land for over forty minutes. I toss my cell on the coffee table as I rise to answer the door. I look through the peephole and see Sierra standing there, staring to her right, toward Jett's house.

"I brought tequila," she squeals when I open the door, holding up two bottles of Jose Cuervo.

"Good thing I settled on Mexican for dinner."

I usher her in and shut and lock the door behind me. Sierra heads straight for the kitchen to grab some shot glasses and pours us both one. The liquid burns a path down my throat and settles like a lead balloon in my stomach. I realize I haven't eaten since breakfast and know I need to rectify that.

"I'm gonna order dinner. Any special requests?" I ask Sierra as I pull up the online ordering app on my cell.

"Nope. My usual is fine," she responds after downing a second shot and slamming the glass on the counter.

Once the food is ordered, we settle on the couch. I hand Sierra the remote so she can pick the movie, but she waves it away.

"No movie tonight." When I open my mouth to speak, she holds her hand up to silence me. "Em, we haven't just *talked* in forever. And we have so freaking much to talk about."

I turn sideways and lean against the arm rest. I stare at Sierra knowing that she's right but not sure *how* to talk about what I'm sure she *wants* to talk about.

Don't be ridiculous. She's your best friend and you can talk to her about anything.

"So, spill."

"There's nothing to spill."

"Bullshit," Sierra counters. "It's been a week since you slept with Jett. I've been so busy getting things wrapped up for the end of the school year that we haven't talked much. Spillage needs to happen, and it needs to happen now." She reaches out and grips my hands in hers. "Please? I'm begging you. I spend all my time with children and haven't had sex in over a month. Let me live vicariously through you."

I snort out a laugh at her antics, but inside I'm doing a little dance because I can't remember the last time my social life was better than Sierra's. Before I launch into details of the past week, I pour myself another shot and down it quickly, letting the liquid fortify me.

Just as I'm about to spill, the doorbell rings and our dinner is delivered. We fix our plates in the kitchen and settle back on the couch. When my plate is almost empty, I set it on the coffee table and turn to face Sierra again.

"Best sex of my life."

Sierra chews faster and swallows the food in her mouth before a huge grin forms. "I knew it!" Her voice drops to a whisper. "Is he, ya know? Big everywhere?"

"You're nuts, you know that don't you?"

"I do. Now, answer the damn question?"

"Yep. Everywhere."

Sierra and I erupt into laughter. It's been so long since I laughed hard enough that my stomach hurts. We spend the next few hours giggling like schoolgirls, drinking tequila, and talking about every guy we've ever slept with, not leaving out a single detail. Eventually we run out of stories and the mood shifts, becomes somber.

"I need to tell you something, Si," I start when I can no longer stand to be quiet.

She looks at me with questions in her eyes, and I know she's drunk. So am I, for that matter. Which is why this is the best time to tell her. Because there's a chance that, come morning, her memory of the conversation will be as distant as her last sexual escapade.

I fill Sierra in on what Jett and I discovered about Len and his connection to Lee. I explain how the riot was planned and executed with the sole purpose of Lee escaping and me being sold. She's appropriately shocked and predictably angry that I'm just now telling her, but she holds in her thoughts until I'm done. Then, she lets it fly.

"Why the fuck didn't you tell me any of this earlier? You tell me everything, but not this?" She stands and starts to pace. "And now you're letting them use you as bait? Your fucking picture is out there, being drooled over by God only knows who and—"

"Stop!" I shout. Sierra freezes mid stride, and her jaw drops open. "Look, I'm sorry I didn't tell you sooner. But I still don't quite have my head wrapped around it, and then add in my... well, whatever you want to call my *thing* with Jett and I'm simply trying to get through a minute at a time. The last thing I need is my best friend judging me and making me feel like an even bigger piece of shit."

Sierra flinches as if I physically struck her. "I... Jesus, I'm not judging you." She crosses her arms over her chest and blows out a breath. "I want you to be safe. I want you to *feel* safe."

"I do feel safe," I assure her. "More than you know."

"Okay." She shrugs her shoulders.

"Look, I'm sorry I didn't tell you." I close the distance between us. "I love you and I just hate that you worry about me all the time. I used to be fearless and lived a pretty carefree life. Now, ever since the riot, it seems it's one thing after another."

"Em, it won't always be like that." Sierra wraps her arms around me in a hug. "I mean, you've come a long way since meeting, or reconnecting, with Jett. He's good for you."

"He really is."

"Just promise me one thing," she says as she grips my shoulders and leans back to look me in the eyes.

"What's that?"

"That you'll be careful. And that when this is all over, you won't hide away anymore and you'll really give this thing with Jett a chance."

"That was three things," I tease her.

"Fine." She chuckles. "Promise me three things."

It's not a hard promise to make. Being reckless isn't an option and neither is going back to the way things were before Jett moved in next door. I take a deep breath as a realization slams into me. I don't *want* to go back to the way things were. I don't want to go back to not having Jett in my life. And I sure as hell don't want to cower like some fragile flower. I'm not that person, the person I let myself become. Not anymore.

"Promise."

24

JETT

"We need to talk."

Sierra's tone warns of anger that's threatening to unleash itself. I guess Emma told her what we're doing to catch Jeffrey Lee and Len Harden. I shove my fingers through my hair in a gesture I now associate with situations that make me slightly uncomfortable.

"Can we talk inside or are you going to make me stay on the porch like a dog?" There's heat in my words, a defense mechanism no doubt.

Sierra steps aside to let me enter. When I step into Emma's living room, I make note of the fact that she's nowhere to be seen. I glance toward the steps and have to fight the urge to go upstairs and see her. Something tells me that I need to deal with Sierra first.

"Answers first," she says, as if reading my thoughts.

"What do you want to know?" I ask, resigned to the conversation.

"What in the ever-loving hell possessed you to use her as bait?"

Okay. So we're jumping right into the deep end.

"Not that it matters, but it wasn't my idea." I stalk past her to get some coffee. The counter is littered with takeout containers and several empty bottles of tequila. When my mug is full, I turn to go back to the living room and am surprised to see Sierra standing in the doorway with her arms crossed over her chest and tapping her foot. "Next question."

"How can you be sure that nothing will happen to her?"

"I protect what's mine," I respond, as if that says it all.

"And Emma is yours?" She arches a brow.

I think about that question a little longer than she'd like, based on the sighs coming from her side of the room. *Is Emma mine?* Yes. *Does Emma want to be mine?* I have no fucking clue.

"Yeah, I guess she is."

"You guess? You *guess?!*"

I blow out a breath, my own anger rising. "Sierra, I appreciate that she's your best friend. Clearly you love her like a sister. But I lo—" I slam my mouth shut and swallow a few times to regain my train of thought. "I like her. A lot. I don't care what it takes, I will keep her out of harm's way. And as far as my feelings toward her, that's between Emma and me."

Sierra appears to mull over my words, and after several silent, tense moments, she gives a sharp nod and whirls around and returns to the living room to sit on the couch. I follow her and sit down.

"Look, I'm not going to lie to you and tell you that this whole thing is one hundred percent risk free. It's not. But despite all of my objections, it's what she wants. I don't like it any more than you do, but at the end of the day, it's her decision. Not mine. Or yours."

Leaning her head back on the couch, she lets her eyes slide closed. I watch her, wondering if she's going to say anything and she doesn't make me wait long.

"You weren't here when everything turned to shit. That riot? It broke her. Shattered her into a million tiny pieces until she was unrecognizable. I've watched her try to put the pieces back together and fail. More times than I can count. And then you came along. Or came back or whatever." She waves her hand around dismissively. "In the last few weeks, I've seen glimpses of the old Emma. The Emma who loves life and isn't afraid of her shadow. Don't get me wrong, she's still scared. But it's not so bad with you around."

"She's stronger than you think," I assure her.

"Oh, I know she is. But does she?"

"I'm working on that."

"I can't lose her." A tear escapes and rolls down her cheek. "You can't let anything, or anyone, hurt her." She swipes at the wetness and lifts her head to pin me with a hard stare. "Do you hear me? *Nothing.* She won't survive it. Not mentally anyway."

"Nothing is going to happen to her. You have my word."

I just pray that my word is as good as I think it is.

∼

"Don't. Stop."

Emma's demand seems to echo in the steam surrounding our bodies. I pound into her from behind, one hand squeezing her hip and the other pinning her arms above her head. When my balls draw tight, I release her arms and shift my attention to her clit.

"Come with me, Em," I growl.

Her walls spasm, and that's all it takes to catapult me over the edge and into oblivion. Emma cries out her release, and when we both float back down, she collapses into my arms. I manage to hold her up despite my own weakened and highly satisfied state.

"I hope we didn't wake Sierra up," she says as we're drying off.

"We didn't. She already went home."

"What?" Emma's gaze cuts to mine. "She never leaves before I get up."

"She was pretty hungover." Emma's face reddens at my words. "I think she just wanted to sleep it off in her own bed." I make the decision to not tell her about my conversation with Sierra. Emma's smart and no doubt knows how worried her friend is. No need to bring it up.

"Makes sense, I guess."

She shrugs her shoulders as if it's no big deal, but the emotion that flashes in her eyes says otherwise. Hurt, confusion, sadness. Needing to take away her pain, I step behind her and wrap my arms around her waist. Our eyes meet in the mirror, and I smile.

"She's fine, doll." I nuzzle her behind her ear. "Stop worrying."

Finally, she smiles and it reaches her eyes. "Okay."

"So, Miss Jordan, what's on the agenda today?" I ask as I get dressed.

She draws her bottom lip between her teeth before answering. The move is sexy as hell, and I have to remind my dick that he's not in charge.

"Are you up for a drive?" she asks.

"Sure. Anything you want."

"I just kinda want to get out of here for a while. There's this place I used to go when I needed to clear my head. I haven't been there in a long time, but I think, with you, I'm ready to go back."

"I'm good with whatever, Em. I need to make sure

Freedom has food and water before we leave, but after that, I'm all yours."

"Why don't we take Freedom with us? It's outdoors and I think she'd love it."

"Are you sure?"

"Of course."

"Okay."

When we finish up at Emma's house, she locks up and we walk next door to get Freedom and some of her toys to play with in the car. I'm not sure how far we're going, but I want Freedom to have something to occupy her during the drive.

"Do you want me to drive?" I ask her, knowing I'll be more comfortable in the Impala because there's more room.

"You don't mind?" She tilts her head as if studying me to see if I'm real.

"Not at all." I snag my keys off the hook by the door, and with Freedom prancing at my feet, ready to go, I motion for Emma to proceed me outside.

Freedom dances around my feet as we walk to the car, almost tripping me several times, and Emma throws her head back and laughs. The sound throws me off guard, and I stop in my tracks to stare.

"What?" she asks, running her fingers through her hair and swiping at her face. "Do I have something on me?"

"No." I shake my head. "You're perfect."

She snorts and opens the passenger door before I can unstick my feet and open it for her. When she climbs in, I force myself to move and shut the door behind her. Freedom follows me around the front, to the driver's side.

Emma gives me directions as I navigate through traffic, and an hour later we're on back roads and heading north. She hasn't told me where our final destination is, but I find I'm enjoying not knowing.

We make small talk and keep the conversation lighthearted. Emma tells me stories about her and Sierra when they were younger, and I hang on to every word. She talks about her brother and his wife, her parents and her first kiss. Jealousy floods my system at the thought of another man tasting her lips. I clench and unclench my fingers on the steering wheel.

"What's wrong?" she asks and tilts her head to indicate my hands.

"I... nothing." I force myself to relax. "Are we almost there?"

"Yes." She looks out the front window. "In another mile or two you're gonna take a left. Now, what's wrong?" she asks again.

I look at her and sigh. "I don't share." My tone is grittier than I like, but I can't help it.

"Okay." She draws out the word. "Not sure what that's supposed to—"

"Women," I snap. "I don't share women. I... the thought of you kissing someone else..." I shake my head to clear it. "I don't share."

She's silent for several seconds, and it's deafening. She breaks the silence with a very unladylike snort.

"Oh my God! You're jealous," she accuses, with surprise in her voice.

"No," I rush to argue. "No, I'm... Fine." I shoot her a glance. "Yes, I'm jealous."

"You do realize that my first kiss was in middle school, right?" She turns away from me to look out her window. "Before you, there was no one for a very long time."

I reach across the seat and pick up her hand, giving it a squeeze. "I'm sorry."

Emma flips her hand over and laces her fingers with mine. "Nothing to be sorry for."

She instructs me to turn right, and when I do, we pass

several trees on either side of the road and come to a clearing. For as far as I can see, the ocean stretches out before us and I lose my breath. I've been to the ocean before, and usually I'm not a fan, but this is different. This is Emma's spot and almost as breathtaking as she is.

"C'mon," she says as she hops out of the car. "We'll walk the rest of the way."

"This isn't it?" I ask.

I let Freedom out and attach the leash to her collar. She darts ahead of me, clearly wanting to catch up with Emma.

"Nope," Emma calls over her shoulder.

Freedom and I catch up to the woman who has stolen my heart. Emma grabs my hand and tugs me down a small embankment. When we hit the beach, we both stop to take our socks and shoes off. My toes sink into the sand, and I glance at Emma. Her head is tilted back, and she's stretching her arms above her head.

"I've missed this."

"I can see why."

I stare at the pulse point at her throat and am so tuned to her that I notice it slowing down the more relaxed she becomes. I reach out and wrap my hand around her neck and pull her to me for a kiss. When our lips touch, scorching heat zings through my veins and goes straight to my cock. I linger for a few minutes before letting her go.

"What was that for?"

"I need a reason to kiss you?" I tease.

"No." Her smile is lazy. "In fact, you can kiss me anytime you want, Jett."

"Good to know."

We hold each other's stare a little longer before she shakes her hand and grabs my hand again. She drags me down the beach until we reach what appears to be a hole in the embankment. The closer we get, the more I realize it's more like a little cubby hole, a perfect cut out that looks to have been made for clearing one's mind and lazy afternoon naps.

"Wow. This is great."

Emma drops to her knees and crawls in the cubby. She flips around and sits on her ass, leaning back against the earthen wall. I follow suit and loop Freedom's leash around a branch nearby. Freedom quickly lays down and gets comfortable in the shade.

"It's a long way to drive sometimes but coming here always makes me feel better."

"How'd you find it?"

Emma scans the horizon. "We used to come here when I was a kid. My parents would take random days off in the summer and declare them 'sand days'." She smiles at the memory. "It was their version of a snow day for school. They'd wake my brother and I up and we'd have ten minutes to get ready to go. Elijah and I would race to see who could make it to the car first. We'd stop for breakfast on our way up here and then we'd spend the day swimming and building sandcastles."

"Sounds like some great memories."

"They are. As I got older, I wanted to play less and less and craved time for myself. I found this spot and would sit here and daydream or read or write in my diary. I always felt, I don't know… refreshed I guess is the right word. This was like my own personal charging pod or something."

We sit there and simply enjoy the sights and sounds. The waves crashing, the kids laughing down the beach, Freedom's snoring. At some point, Emma moved to sit between my legs and her head is resting on my chest. It feels right, being with her, having her near.

"Did you have a place you'd go when you were a kid? Back in Indiana?"

My body tenses at her question, and I know she feels it because she sits up and turns to face me. I try not to look at her, not to let her see what I know is reflected in my eyes when I think about my childhood.

"Uh, yeah, I did." I rub the back of my neck. "*We* did. Sort of. Harrison and me. We, uh, had a treehouse in our backyard. My dad built it after I was born. Always said that brothers need a place to bond." I smile remembering the hours upon hours spent with Harrison in that thing. "When we were little, we used to sit in it and play with our matchbox cars. I always had the cop car and he had a little red car that he'd make me chase. As we got older, it turned into a place we'd go to get away from our parents, and then it became the spot we'd take girls." I laugh at the memory of it all.

"Sounds nice."

"It was. But then..." Suddenly my throat feels clogged, and it's hard to breathe. I squeeze my eyes shut against the onslaught of memories that race through my mind like they're playing on a movie reel. I clear my throat and force myself to continue. "When Harrison died, my dad torched it and the tree it was in. He got a pretty big fine from the fire department, but he didn't care."

"How did Harrison die?" Emma asks softly.

I feel her fingers brush against mine, the touch featherlight but somehow it grounds me in the here and now.

"He was murdered. He got tangled up in the wrong crowd, started selling dope and one night the sale went bad." My vision blurs as I recall that night. "I remember waking up to my mother screaming. I ran downstairs to see what was going on, and she was on her knees and my dad was standing there, staring at nothing. I knew, without anyone saying a word, what happened. I was supposed to go with Harrison that night, but at the last minute, I backed out.

Maybe if I'd been there, I could have done something. Saved him."

"If you'd been there, you'd likely be dead too." Emma's voice is soothing as she wraps her body around mine and holds me while I cry.

I let the tears flow, tears that I've held in since my world burned to the ground as easily as that tree house had. Time passes, but Emma doesn't let go. When the tears subside, I take several deep breaths to regain my composure. Emma loosens her hold but doesn't break contact.

"That's why you joined the DEA," she remarks. "Because of your brother. Because of what happened to Harrison."

I nod. "I always blamed myself for not going with him, for not telling my parents what he was doing. That was my way of making up for my mistakes. For *his* mistakes. Not only did I lose Harrison that night, but I lost my parents too. They were never the same. They could barely look at me. Harrison and I looked a lot alike, and I guess it was too painful for them. Jesus, I don't even know the last time we spoke. It was before I went undercover."

"Where are they now?"

"Dead," I respond, my tone hollow. "They died in a car accident while I was in the cage."

"Damn." A glance at Emma reveals tears streaking down her cheeks. "That's awful. I'm so sorry, Jett. I'm sorry that you've been through so much."

"I've lost everyone." I lock eyes with her, hold her stare for as long as I can. "But all of it led me to you. Somehow, all that pain, all that heartache, all that *loss*... You're the light at the end of a very dark tunnel."

"I don't..." She shakes her head, her eyes wide with questions. "How can you think that? With everything going on, I'm no bright light. More like a black void leading to Hell."

"You're so wrong, doll." I cup her cheek. "I know things

are crazy right now and we didn't exactly meet under normal circumstances, but you make my life better."

"But—"

I press a finger to her lips, silencing her. "No buts, Emma." I remove my finger and lean my forehead against hers. "Answer me this. Are you happy? If you strip away all of the crazy bullshit, are you happy? Do I make you happy?"

"Yes," she responds without hesitation.

"Then let's just hold onto that."

Emma lets out a deep sigh. "Okay, Jett."

She turns in my arms and rests her back to my front. Images of my brother, of my parents, continue to run through my head, but rather than painful ones, they're memories that make me smile and remember the good times.

It's a long time before we move from our spot in the little natural cubby. As we walk to the car, I can't help but feel a little lighter, a little less burdened. For the first time in years, I feel content because I know I'm exactly where I'm meant to be and with who I'm meant to be with.

Why, then, can't I rid myself of that other feeling? That one that has me on a razor thin edge, just waiting to be pushed back into the darkness?

25

EMMA

Two weeks have gone by since I became an item to be sought after and purchased, like the latest piece of technology that everyone just has to have. Slade has been by several times to go over details with Jett. For the most part, they keep to themselves, but Jett always fills me in afterward. He seems to understand that not knowing is somehow just as awful as knowing.

"Are you sure you're up for this?" Jett runs his hands up and down my arms.

"I'm sure." Slade asked to meet with both of us today, and ever since he called Jett, I haven't been able to stop pacing. "When's he supposed to be here?"

A knock on the door startles me and answers my question. Jett lets Slade in, and the three of us gather around Jett's kitchen table. While Slade sets up his laptop, I fidget with my hands under the table.

"Can I get either of you something to drink?" I ask, hating the silence.

"I'd love some coffee," Slade says without looking up from his computer.

"Jett?"

"Thanks, doll. Coffee sounds great."

I rush to fill two mugs, and when I return to the table, they're both staring intently at the laptop. Jett's face is red and twisted in rage while Slade's expression is a bit harder to read.

"What are you looking at?" I ask as I hand their mugs to them.

Slade looks up from the computer, pity in his eyes. His face softens, and he and Jett exchange a look before he returns his attention to me. "Why don't you sit down and we can get into the reason I wanted to talk to you?"

I plop down in the chair with a thud. I knew this meeting was going to be something I didn't like, and my fears are confirmed more with each passing second.

Slade takes a deep breath, and his eyes narrow. "There's been a lot of interest in your, shall we say, listing, since it went live." I cringe at his statement. "I've got an alert set up so that I'm notified any time there's action on it. So, if someone bids, I know right away."

Jett must note the confusion on my face, and he clarifies. "This particular site is set up much like eBay. A buyer can bid on *items* or they can buy them outright. They can also mark a listing so they can watch it."

"Okay." I swallow the bile that's threatening. "I'm guessing by this meeting and the looks on your faces that I've been sold."

"No. Not exactly." Slade shifts in his chair, looking uncomfortable. He turns to Jett, who's pacing behind Slade's chair like a caged animal. "Sit the hell down. You're driving me nuts back there."

Jett glares at him but does as he's told. "What do you mean, not exactly," he sneers. He balls his hands into fists on the table, and his knuckles turn white from the pressure.

"I want to speed things up a bit." Slade holds his hand up to silence Jett when he rushes to his feet. "Hear me out." Jett sits again and slams his fists on the table, sloshing coffee over the rims of the mugs. "I want to buy Emma."

Slade says the words so quickly that they almost don't register. Almost.

"Absolutely not!" Jett shouts. "It's bad enough that we're using her as bait, but I refuse to put her in a position where she actually has to face them."

"Think about it, Jett. They don't even have her. Once she's sold, it'll force their hand and they'll have to come after her so they can produce her to the buyer. We'll know they're coming and we'll be ready for them."

"Not happening," Jett seethes. "It's too—"

"Enough!" I yell as I jump to my feet. Both of them slam their mouths closed and stare at me with wide eyes. "First of all, quit talking about me like I'm not right here. Second," I focus my gaze on Jett. "I appreciate that you want to protect me, but this is my choice, not yours."

"But—"

"No buts, Jett." I lower my gaze and take a deep breath. When I refocus on his eyes, they're blurry from the tears in mine. "I'm not Harrison." I hate the hurt I see at my words, so I close the distance between us and wrap my arms around his waist. "Protecting me isn't going to bring him back. That's not how things work."

Jett's arms come around me, and his hold is so tight it makes it difficult to breathe.

"Jett, I need you to trust me," Slade says from behind us. "I get it, man. I really do. I hated when Brandie was the target of all this evil, but at the end of the day, she's alive and one more of the bad guys is off the streets."

Jett takes a deep breath, his body shuddering as he blows it out. He steps back and speaks to Slade but never breaks eye contact with me. "Fine. But there's no way in hell I'm not going to be involved in every single step."

"Done," Slade agrees.

Silence ensues. I imagine we're all trying to come to terms with what has been decided and think of ways to pull it off. Jett is the first one to speak.

"Once she's *sold*, someone will come for her." He glances at me. "You'll need to stay at your house, but I'll always be there. When they come, we'll be ready."

I nod in agreement and swallow before looking to Slade. "Buy me."

∼

"I hate this."

Jett hasn't stopped voicing his concern about this plan since Slade left. It was decided that Slade would stay at Jett's house—with the agreement of his fiancé, Brandie—and Jett would stay with me.

"I know." I press my cheek to his bare chest and focus on his heartbeat. "Me too."

"I can't lose you."

I place a kiss on his pec before rising up on my elbow so I can look him in the eye. "You won't."

"I think..." He closes his eyes briefly, and when he opens them, they're dark with need. "No, I know... I love you, Em. So fucking much. If anything happens to you, I don't think I'll survive it like I did with Harrison and my parents."

My pulse races, and my stomach flutters. I lean over and fuse my lips with his, darting my tongue in and out to tempt and tease him. Jett pulls me up to straddle him, and his rigid cock tantalizes my pussy.

I trail my fingers down his torso to the waistband of his boxer briefs. He lifts his hips so I can tug them down his legs, and when he's free, I wrap my hand around him and guide him to my already exposed center. Jett thrusts to meet me and fills me up.

I throw my head back as I ride him, lost in ecstasy.

"Look at me," he growls.

I lower my gaze. Jett cups my cheeks and pulls me toward him for a bruising kiss. The rhythm of his tongue matches the thrusts of our hips. There's no denying the physical chemistry, but, following his pronouncement, there's an emotional connection that's more prevalent than before.

Jett reaches between our bodies and rubs fast circles over my throbbing clit. Waves of pleasure pulse through me, and I explode from the inside out. His cock swells and he shouts out my name as his cum fills me.

I collapse against him in a sweaty heap and trace lazy circles on his chest.

"Jett?"

"Hmm?"

"I love you too."

26

JETT

"What the hell?"

Emma is pressed against me, sleeping peacefully, and I try not to wake her as I get out of bed to investigate the noise that woke me. The second the floor creaks under my weight, I freeze and glance over my shoulder. Emma mumbles in her sleep and curls into a ball, facing the wall. I breathe a sigh of relief and continue toward the door, taking my gun from the nightstand with me.

Silence greets me when I step into the hall, and I pause to listen for any sign that I wasn't hearing things. Nothing. I clear each room upstairs before making my way downstairs.

The front door is still locked and the living room is empty. I begin to question my sanity as I head for the kitchen, but just as I step through the doorway, I hear the noise again. I strain to listen, but I can't make out what it is or where it's coming from.

"What are you doing?"

I whirl around and aim my weapon. Emma's frightened eyes stare back and me, and her hands are raised in the air. I drop my arm and blow out the breath that was trapped in my throat at the sound of her voice. "Jesus, don't do that. I could've killed you."

My heart thunders in my chest, and I try to breathe normally. Emma slowly walks toward me, and when she's a few inches away, she flattens her hands against my chest.

"I'm sorry I scared you. I woke up and you weren't in bed. I just wanted to see where you were."

"A noise woke me. I was just checking it out."

"What kind of noise?" she asks with alarm tinging her voice.

"I don't know. But everything seems to be fine. Maybe I'm just on edge."

Emma steps back and glances around the room as if searching for something I couldn't find. Her eyes land on the window over the sink, and her shoulders tense. I follow her stare and that's when I see it. The window is open, barely, and I try to recall if it was open before we went to bed or not.

"That wasn't…" Emma swallows. "It wasn't open earlier."

"Are you sure?"

"Positive. I always double check everything. It was closed."

"Was it locked?"

"Yes. At least I think it was."

I step up to the sink and lean over it to peer out the window. There's no light, other than that of the moon, so nothing has tripped the motion sensors. I close the window and lock it before pulling the curtains together.

"I've cleared the house, so we're good. We should probably try to go back to bed."

I grab Emma's hand and usher her back to the living room. When we reach the steps, an intense pain radiates at the back of my head. As I whirl around, I'm immediately struck again, this time at my temple.

Emma's screams surround me as I fight to maintain consciousness and remain upright. Another blow knocks me to the floor, and my vision blurs, making it impossible to identify my attacker.

"I'm sorry," I manage to croak before the blackness surrounds me.

∽

Emma

"Jett!" I scream and drop to my knees next to him.

"Get the fuck up," Len barks, yanking me to my feet by my hair.

A whimper escapes past my lips. "Please, Len. Please don't hurt—"

Pain shoots through my cheek when Len backhands me. My head whips to the side, and my hand flies to my face. Heat radiates from my skin. Len slams something against my chest and whirls me around.

"Tie him up," he demands. I glance at the handcuffs and rope dangling from my fingers but make no move to do as I'm told. Len tangles his fingers in my hair and pulls my head back until I feel his mouth against my ear. "Don't underestimate me, Emma. You won't like what happens if you do."

I try to reconcile the man in front of me with the awkward prison doctor I worked with. It's like I'm face to face with Dr. Jekyll and Mr. Hyde. Not wanting to experience any more of Len's wrath, I bend down and sit on my haunches next to Jett and slowly begin to tie him up.

"You won't get away with this," I say over my shoulder. It's the middle of the night and Slade is probably sleeping next door, making my statement an empty threat. But I'll try anything to stop this madness.

"We'll see about that," he quips.

Once Jett is secure, Len pulls me to my feet and jams what I can only assume is a gun into my back. He guides me out the front door, down my steps and shoves me into the back of a waiting van.

A quick glance around me intensifies my fear, and my dinner from the night before threatens to make an appearance. Inside the van is a cage made out of steel pipes. It reminds me of the jail cells I spent so much time around. There's a padlock on the cage, blocking me from getting to the back door and escaping.

As much as I don't want to, I look at Len. His eyes are gleaming orbs of evil, and his eerie smile only solidifies the look. He slams the door closed, and I hear metal scraping from the outside followed by another door opening and closing, and then the engine rumbles to life.

There are no windows to look out of to see where we're going. I lean against the side panel and let the tears fall. *How did this happen?* I don't waste much time on that line of thinking. It won't get me out of this mess.

Wiping the salty wetness from my face, I concentrate on the sounds that surround me. Every bump in the road, every turn that has me struggling to stay upright. Music filters through from the front of the van and the lyrics of 'Every Breath You Take' wash over me. Somehow, the love song, in my current situation, sends shivers down my spine.

The song plays on repeat for the remainder of the drive. By the time we stop, I have no idea how many turns Len's made and my shivering isn't only from the music.

I crawl toward the back of the van and wrap my numb fingers around the bars. I cock my head and listen as Len's voice mixes with another. Recognition slams into me, knocking me backward and onto my ass.

Time seems to slow as I watch the door open and two men come into view. I scramble away from them, but Jeffrey Lee reaches between the bars and grabs my ankle.

"Ah, Miss Jordan. We meet again."

27

JETT

"Jesus, what happened?"

My limbs tingle as sensation returns after Slade unlocks the cuffs and cuts the rope around my ankles. I jump to my feet and press a hand to the back of my head, my fingers coming away sticky with blood.

"Jett, answer me," Slade demands. "What happened?"

I shove him out of the way, ignoring his question. "Emma!" I call out as I run upstairs. "Emma!" Her room is empty, as is the rest of the house.

"Jett," Slade shouts, stopping me in my tracks back in the living room.

"They took her." My chest heaves with every breath that I force in and out of my lungs. "I have to find her."

I throw open the front door, only to have Slade's hand flatten against the barrier and slam it closed.

"You need to fill me the fuck in so we can do this right."

I glare at him. "They got the drop on me. Took her right out from under my nose."

"Who?"

"Fuck, I didn't see who it was. But it had to be Lee or

Len." I slam my fist into the wall. "Goddammit! I knew they were coming, and they still got her."

"It's not your fault," Slade says quietly. "Besides, you know they're not going to hurt her. She's product to them. A money-maker. They kill her, they lose the buyer."

His words make sense, but they do little to tame the beast in me that's raging to get out. I begin to pace, trying to come up with a way to get to Emma, to get her away from two psychopaths.

"I think our best bet is to wait." Slade shuffles on the balls of his feet. "I got an anonymous email that said I'd be contacted with information on the pick-up of my *purchase*. Now that they have her, they're not going to wait long. They want their money."

As if on cue, his phone beeps with a notification. He pulls it from his pocket and glances at the screen.

"Read it out loud," I demand.

"Bring the money to the abandoned warehouse by the pier. Be there at noon. Not a minute before. Your product will be waiting for you there. I hope you're good at picking locks."

"What the fuck does that mean?" I snarl as I snatch the phone from his hand to read it myself.

"It means," he starts as he takes his cell back. "You're gonna get her back."

I shove shaky fingers through my hair and start to pace again. Why are they doing the exchange in the middle of the day? And why the fuck do we need to be able to pick a lock? It makes no sense to me that Emma is just going to be left there, unattended. Question after question plagues me, and I feel like we're missing something. But what?

"I'm going to go grab my shit from your place. Why don't you come with me and get your gear? You can let Freedom out, and we'll get ready to head out."

I give a curt nod and follow Slade outside, pulling Emma's door shut behind me and locking it. When we reach my house, I head straight for the basement, where all of my tactical gear is stored.

With my arms loaded, I climb the steps and hear Slade on the phone. I catch the end of his conversation, and it sounds like he's getting a team to the pier to scope things out. When he ends the call, I ask him as much.

"A team will be there shortly." At my questioning stare, he holds a hand up. "Jett, they know what they're doing. They know how to blend in and not be seen. It'll be fine."

"It better be," I growl.

Freedom rubs up against my leg, and I glance at her. Freedom usually has a way of calming me and I wish it were working now.

"C'mon, girl."

I take Freedom out to the backyard and watch her do her thing. As I watch her, I can't help but wonder if I'll ever be able to share this with Emma. My heart bleeds at the thought of never seeing her again, of never getting to see where life takes us.

I shake off my melancholy and get Freedom settled once we're back inside. It doesn't take long for Slade and me to be ready to leave and a glance at the clock tells me that it's almost go time.

I take in Slade's appearance. He's wearing a suit in an effort to appear like the wealthy man he's supposed to be. I know he has a bullet-proof vest underneath, but the expensive suit covers it nicely. It's almost as if it was tailored to fit like a glove over whatever gear he needed underneath.

"Let's go."

We take Slade's vehicle, as he's the buyer and we don't want to tip Lee or Len off that he's not alone. He follows the

GPS directions, and the closer we get to our destination, the more my stomach twists into knots.

The warehouse comes into view, and I note the empty parking lot. I scan the surrounding area but see no one. For the first time since I was pulled from sleep, I feel like luck is on our side.

"It's quiet," Slade murmurs. "Too quiet."

Slade parks next to a door on the side of the building. There's an ominous sign taped to the door that reads 'Enter here'. The paper is stark white, which tells me that the sign was placed there just for us.

"Let me go in first, scope things out."

Slade steps out of the vehicle, and it takes everything in me to sit still and wait. He grabs the duffel bag out of the back seat, the one that has his 'payment' in it. He looks around as he makes his way to the door, and when he opens it, it squeaks on its hinges. Slade steps across the threshold, keeping his foot in place to keep the door from closing. I hold my breath as I wait for the signal to join him. He doesn't keep me waiting long.

Slade glances over his shoulder at me and gives a nod, letting me know it's okay to get out of the vehicle. His face is an angry red, and rather than wait for me, he drops the bag to hold the door open and rushes inside.

I waste no time, and when I cross the threshold, my blood boils. There's a small cage in the middle of the empty room, and Emma's lying on her side, curled up in the fetal position. I rush to the makeshift cell, ignoring Slade's protests.

"Emma," I call to her. I reach through the bars and shake her foot. "Emma, wake up."

She stirs and when she rolls over, my stomach drops. Her lip is split, and dried blood covers her chin. Her cheek is an angry red, and her left eye is swollen shut.

"Get your team in here," I shout at Slade. "And paramedics."

"On it."

"Emma." I shake her again in an effort to get her to come fully awake. "C'mon, doll. I'm here. I need you to wake up."

She stirs some more, and her eyes flutter open. When she sees me, she seems to snap out of it and scrambles to her knees.

"Jett?"

"Yeah, doll. It's me." I grab her hand and squeeze it. "We're gonna get you outta here."

"Okay. I don't know where they went after they jabbed—"

A sound from across the room catches my attention, and I rise to my feet, whirling around as I do. I aim my weapon at the two figures entering the space.

"I told you he'd come." Len's tone is matter of fact and gives away no indication that he's worried that he's been caught.

"Shut up," Jeffrey Lee shouts at him.

Lee struts toward me, showing no fear of the gun trained at his head. When he's a foot in front of me, he smiles.

"Last time I saw you, Storm, you were trying to rescue Miss Jordan."

"I'm pretty sure I did rescue her," I reply.

"Yes, I suppose that's true. But then again," he hitches a thumb over his shoulder toward the cage. "Look where she is now."

"Quit messing around Lee," Len yells. "That fucking cop already called his team. We don't have long."

Lee tilts his head. "This is why I don't like depending on other people. They whine and demand and always want to do things their way."

"I guess you thought you'd have it made after your sister

JETT'S GUARD

died, then." I try to keep him talking, keep him occupied and his attention away from Emma.

"Sapphire wasn't my sister!" Spit flies from his lips. "She was a means to an end. Unfortunately, things didn't work quite how I'd hoped. But that's all going to change today."

I watch Len out of the corner of my eye, and he steps closer to the cage, reaching in to try to grab a hold of Emma. She dodges his grasp, and the action only fuels his crazy.

"This would have been so much easier if you'd just gone on a date with me. Maybe then I wouldn't have been forced to help Lee." Len pulls a knife from a sheath at his waist. "But no," he jeers, waving the knife around as he talks. "You kept brushing me off. And then, to make matters worse, you went and slept with that, that..." He points the knife in my direction and stammers. "That motherfucking *thing*!"

Spit flies from Len's mouth as he rages. Lee listens to every word Len spews and appears bored. Len goes on and on about how this is all Emma's fault, and before I can even register what's happening, Lee pulls a gun from his jacket, whirls around and squeezes the trigger.

Len's knife falls from his grasp as he drops to the concrete floor. The knife slides away from his body, towards the cage, and blood pools under him from the hole in his head. Emma stares at him, her eyes wide and frantic.

"You're welcome," Lee says when he turns back around to face me.

"What the fuck for?" I snarl.

"For making the world a safer place."

Holy fuck! This guy is crazier than we thought.

"Okay, so Len's dead. That's great." I try to keep my tone light, conversational. "Makes taking you out so much easier."

"You'd think that, wouldn't you?"

Lee takes a step back and reaches through the cage to grab Emma's arm. She tries to lean away, but she's not fast enough. Lee yanks her forward so her cheek slams against the bars, and I see red.

"Let her go," I growl, maintaining my aim with my gun on his head.

"This was supposed to be easy," Lee says. "Lure the buyer here, let him drop the money and then watch as he struggles to get this damn cage open." He looks beyond me. "Take him out from that room over there, and then I get my money and the bitch."

"Sucks when plans don't work out." I shrug. "Now, drop her hand and your weapon and put your hands up."

"Yeah, I don't think so."

Lee raises his gun and points it at me. I squeeze my trigger and multiple shots ring out. Pain sears through my arm at the same time that Lee's body jerks with the force of the bullet tearing through his chest and then falls to the floor. He's still, silent and bloody. Slade rushes forward to check for signs of life, and when he finds none, he shakes his head.

I glare at Lee's dead body and can only hope that it was my bullet that ended his life. Satisfied that all threats have been eliminated, I rush to the lock on the cage and the words in the email resurface.

"Check him for the key," I call to Slade over my shoulder, ignoring the flurry of activity around me from Slade's team.

Slade finds a ring of keys, and the second one I try pops the lock. I throw open the door and pull Emma out. She launches herself at me, running her hands over my face and head, no doubt inspecting my own wounds from earlier.

"I think you're gonna need stitches," Slade comments as he steps toward me and inspects the torn flesh on my arm.

I spare a quick glance at the blood trickling down my arm from where the bullet grazed me, but then I cup Emma's face, as gently as possible, and lean in to capture her lips in a kiss. She hisses at the contact but doesn't pull away. A tap on my shoulder catches my attention, and I break the connection.

"Did you hear a word I just said?" Slade asks.

"Not a damn one." I respond to him but never take my eyes off of Emma.

He chuckles. "Didn't think so." He points to my arm and Emma's face. "Stitches… you both need to be checked out and will likely need stitches."

"Yeah, I'm not going to the hospital," Emma retorts. "I just want to go to Jett's house to shower and crawl into bed and sleep off this nightmare."

"You heard her." I tug her into my arms and hold her close. "The paramedics can check us out, but that's it." I look around the room.

"Fine," Slade huffs out. He bends down to inspect Lee again and then shifts his attention to Len, poking him in the shoulder. "When are you crazy bastards gonna learn not to fuck with our women?" he mumbles as he pokes Len's shoulder.

"I hope you're not expecting an answer," I say.

"Of course not," he scoffs. Slade stands and looks at Emma. "Well, this isn't exactly how I pictured it would happen, but it should be over now."

"Should be?" There's fear in Emma's tone.

"There's always going to be evil in the world. We can't stop them all. But the threat to you is over." He smiles at her.

"He's right, doll."

Emma nods and turns in my arms to survey her surroundings. After a few silent minutes, she takes a deep breath and says to Slade, "I have a question."

"What's that?"

"I assume since I was taken from my house it's a crime scene. But for how long?"

"Shouldn't be more than a day or two. I'll make sure it's as quick as possible. Why?"

Emma turns to me. "Did you mean it before?"

"Mean what?"

"When you said you loved me? Did you mean it? Now that this is over, do you still love me, still want to be with me?" She chews her bottom lip while she waits for my answer.

"Emma, I love you. I will always love you. This," I sweep my arm to encompass the carnage. "Changes nothing."

"Good." She throws her arms around my neck. "Because I'm selling my house and moving in with you and Freedom." The corners of her mouth curve into a grin.

"I love you, Jett 'Storm' Stover."

EPILOGUE

JETT

Two years later...

"I'm home!"

Emma's voice carries through the house as she walks through the front door, same as it does every time she returns from work. I look over my shoulder at our son who's sitting in his highchair next to the counter.

"Hear that, buddy? Mama's home."

I dry my hands on the towel and lift Harrison into my arms. When he was born, Emma insisted we name him after my brother, and I couldn't have been more thrilled.

"Hey, sweet boy," Emma sing-songs when she enters the kitchen.

She stretches her arms out to take Harrison from me, but I move him just out of her reach. "Me first," I say and lean forward for a kiss.

She obliges and I hand her our baby boy. "Were you a

good boy for Daddy today?" she asks him, as if he's going to answer.

"He was great," I say. "But then again, he's always great." I return to the task of loading the dishwasher. "How was your day?"

"Long." My wife lets out a sigh, and I hear the chair scrape across the floor as she pulls it out from the table to sit down. "Sierra is being a pain in my ass and insisted we let the rest of the staff handle the center while we went shopping."

"What the hell else could you possibly need?" The laughter in my voice is unmistakable.

"That's what I said! I told her that we have everything left from when Harrison was born, but she just keeps saying that she knows this one is gonna be a little girl so we need girly things."

I turn in time to see Emma rub her very pregnant belly. Harrison's head is resting on her shoulder, and he's fighting his drooping eyelids.

"Why don't I put him down in his room and get a bath started for you?" I squat next to her chair so I'm level with her stomach. "Do you wanna relax with Mommy?" I ask the baby bump.

"Ooo, I think that kick means 'yes'." I help Emma to her feet. "And thank you. Between the center, Sierra, and little peanut here," she smiles down at her bump, "I'm beat."

I help Emma to our room and decide to lay Harrison down on a blanket on the bed while I get her situated. Freedom jumps on the bed and lays between him and the edge, forever protecting her best friend.

While I draw Emma a bath, I listen while she talks about the latest teen at the center. "He's really a good kid. His parents are convinced he's running the streets with the wrong crowd, but I think they're just on high alert after they lost their daughter to an overdose."

My heart swells with pride. My beautiful wife came to me a month after everything happened with Len and said she wanted to start a center for troubled teens. A place where they could go to keep them off the streets and away from trouble. I was immediately on board, and we used what remained of my inheritance and the profits from the sale of her house to get it started.

"Has he met with Elijah yet?" I ask, knowing that Emma makes every new teen meet with her brother to review the rules.

"Sure has," she laughs. "Elijah's assessment is that he's just a hurt kid and needs to talk to someone who understands what he's going through. I thought maybe tomorrow you could come in and talk with him."

"I'd be happy to."

I don't work at the center, but I do sometimes go in to talk with any of the kids that might benefit from my story. It's gotten easier to talk about, and that's all because of Emma. She makes life easier.

"Thank you," she says sweetly as she strips her clothes and steps into the hot bath water.

"Anything for you, doll."

I kneel next to the tub and dip a washcloth in the water. Once it's wet, I run it over her body, making sure to pay extra attention to all the spots that turn her on. In a matter of seconds, Emma's moaning and twisting her fingers in my shirt to tug me toward her.

"Harrison's asleep," she says just before pressing a quick kiss on my lips. "I'm wet." Another kiss. "And needy." She leans back in the water and lets her knees fall open. "You should come take care of that."

I get my clothes off so fast and join my horny wife in the steaming water. I shift her around so she's straddling me and spend the next hour working her into a frenzy of desperation, only letting her fall over that edge when I am close enough to join her.

Two weeks later, Emma jokes with the doctor that it's my fault that our daughter, Ivy Lynn, entered the world a little early.

ABOUT THE AUTHOR

Andi Rhodes is an author whose passion is creating romance from chaos in all her books! She writes MC (motorcycle club) romance with a generous helping of suspense and doesn't shy away from the more difficult topics. Her books can be triggering for some so consider yourself warned. Andi also ensures each book ends with the couple getting their HEA! Most importantly, Andi is living her real life HEA with her husband and their boxers.

For access to release info, updates, and exclusive content, be sure to sign up for Andi's newsletter at andirhodes.com.

ALSO BY ANDI RHODES

Broken Rebel Brotherhood

Broken Souls

Broken Innocence

Broken Boundaries

Broken Rebel Brotherhood: Complete Series Box set

Broken Rebel Brotherhood: Next Generation

Broken Hearts

Broken Wings

Broken Mind

Bastards and Badges

Stark Revenge

Slade's Fall

Jett's Guard

Soulless Kings MC

Fender

Joker

Piston

Greaser

Riker

Trainwreck

Squirrel

Gibson

Satan's Legacy MC

Snow's Angel

Toga's Demons

Magic's Torment